FRIED CHICKEN & FANGS

A Southern Charms Cozy Mystery

BELLA FALLS

Evermore Press

ISBN-10: 198058155X

ISBN-13: 978-1980581550

Cover by Victoria Cooper

❀ Created with Vellum

Also by Bella Falls

A Southern Charms Cozy Mystery Series

Moonshine & Magic: Book 1

Fried Chicken & Fangs: Book 2

Sweet Tea & Spells: Book 3

Lemonade & Love Potions (a short formerly in the Hexes & Ohs Anthology)

For a FREE exclusive copy of the prequel Chess Pie & Choices, sign up for my newsletter!

https://dl.bookfunnel.com/opbg5ghpyb

Share recipes, talk about Southern Charms and all things cozy mysteries, and connect with me by joining my reader group Southern Charms Cozy Companions!

https://www.facebook.com/groups/southerncharmscozycompanions

/

CONTENTS

Preface

The story of *Fried Chicken & Fangs* occurs after the Southern Charms short Lemonade & Love Potions, found in the *Hexes & Ohs* Anthology, where failed cupid Skeeter Jones throws a singles mingle event that goes slightly wrong.

Reading the short isn't necessary, but it will enhance your experience in enjoying Southern Charms Cozy Mystery Book 2.

Chapter One

"I hate you." I glared at Blythe, sitting down next to me, smugness radiating off her.

The bright sun's rays beat down on us, giving me a powerful hankerin' for some sweet tea. But even some of the delicious nectar of the South might not improve my mood.

"Next time, maybe you should volunteer to be on the committee. Then you might not get stuck doing something you don't want to do. Here." One of my closest friends and longtime confidantes pushed a tall cup with a lid and straw into my hand. "Maybe this will make it all better and stop your sulking."

I had been one of the biggest supporters of making changes to Honeysuckle Hollow, and I counted the idea to add a Saturday market open to the magical community at large surrounding our small isolated town as one of my better contributions...behind the scenes. But I would figure out who volunteered my behind to sit at a table with a sign labeled *Lost & Found*. I would find them, and then I would hex their hiney into the next century.

"Not likely," I pouted. "Who's bright idea was it to put me in charge of *this*?" I tore off the sign and waved it in front of my friend's face.

Blythe made little effort to stifle a chuckle. "Someone said that at other farmers' and flea markets they've visited, there's always a *Lost & Found* table. We wanted to be like all the others."

"But who decided to make *me* be in charge of it?" I narrowed my eyes at her. I didn't know how a table like mine worked at markets outside in the human world, but I had a nagging suspicion how it would turn out with me and my tracking powers in charge of things.

She shrugged her shoulders. "Not my place to tell. If you want to join the committee—"

"I am not going to join a group with that name," I interrupted.

"Aw, come on. You know that's not the official name. That's what Henry calls us whenever he hangs out at Harvest Moon," protested my friend.

"He calls you *POOP*. *Posse Of Open Progress*. Nobody should volunteer to be a part of *POOP*. I've said it before, and I'll say it again. Names are important." Taking a sip of sweet tea, I slumped into the back of my chair, giving side eye to the few people lingering in front of my table and reading the sign that Blythe had put back in place.

"The committee doesn't have a name. It's just a group of us the council put together to discuss and help implement new ideas and changes to our sleepy little Southern community. With the upcoming election for the new council seat, you know things are gonna get tense around here." Blythe looked over at the gazebo where others were setting up for the candidate speeches later that evening.

"Yeah," I agreed. "Whenever Nana's stressed, she cooks and bakes up a storm. She's sent so much good food home with me to Tipper's house, I haven't had to fire up the stove once."

"Not Tipper's house. Your house. You need to get used to saying that. It's been long enough, honey bun." My friend rubbed my back. "How's the clean out going, by the way?"

"It's gonna take me a long time to go through all of my great-uncle's things. I don't want to throw anything out that has value." I sighed at the thought of the daunting task. "Beau has actually been a big help."

When I'd offered the plump older vampire and former best friend to my great-uncle the opportunity to continue to stay and live in the house as my roommate, I would have never guessed how much I would appreciate his presence. And not just for his cheerful willingness to sort through all of the stuff that Tipper had hoarded, although my occasional and usually empty threats to kick him out might have been an influencing factor.

Blythe pointed at something. "Uh-oh. Incoming."

Skeeter Johnson bobbed and fluttered in our direction until he hovered up and down in front of us, his wings working overtime to hold up his plump cherub body. The disgraced and unemployed cupid's hangdog face drooped with even more disappointment than usual. "Excuse me, Miss Charli. But I could use your help findin' something." He pointed at the sign.

"What's missing?" I asked. "Did you lose something here at the market?"

He shook his head, the trucker's hat he wore on top of his messy curls shaking off-center. "No, no, Miss Charli. I mean, I could use your skills to help me find a specific item that I seem to have misplaced." He cast his eyes to the ground in shame.

My heart took pity on the poor fella, and I sighed. "Fine. What is it you lost?"

His eyes brightened at my willingness to help. "You see, I have an interview coming up. The supervisor of Cupid Local 303 is willing to reinstate me on a probationary basis."

"That's great. Congratulations." Unable to clap him on the back due to his wings, I held up my fist for him to bump.

He stared at my hand, unwilling to accept my praise, his lower lip trembling. "Except, I lost my quiver." He wrung his small hands together in worry, his eyes darting around to make sure nobody heard his shame.

Having had experience with one of his disasters, I pushed

the tiny troublemaker. "Just the quiver? Or what goes *inside* it as well?"

Any cupid worth his or her salt needed their official equipment. On top of that, having a Cupid's arrow out in the open for anyone to find meant trouble with a capital *T*. The little bugger blushed and averted his eyes in response. Pixie poop.

I stood up, stopping Blythe from yelling at the helpless guy. "Okay, Skeeter. Give me your hand, and I'll see what I can do." I concentrated and gathered my energy and focus, waiting for the touch of his skin.

For a few months, I had been working on building my tracking skills, or *birddoggin'* as my late great-Uncle Tipper used to call it. Before that, I had left my hometown to learn from others with magical talents like mine. When I'd first returned, my practice time got waylaid by a teeny tiny little death curse that almost killed me. My skin had grown much tougher to the odd stares and occasional whispers. Still, after details of how I'd helped solve my great-uncle's murder leaked, most everybody at least respected my peculiar magic.

With the cupid's hands clasped in mine, I gave him instructions to help me. "Picture the items you want. It might help to think about where they were the last time that you saw your things? You got that in your mind?"

Skeeter scrunched his eyes closed. "Think so." The trucker's hat came perilously close to falling off his nodding head.

I closed my eyes, commencing the first steps of

connection. "Concentrate on them," I demanded, following his lead and shutting out the rest of the world.

"Hold on," interrupted Skeeter.

I blinked my eyes open. "What?" I asked in annoyance.

He tilted his head. "Aren't you going to say a rhyme or something? I thought that you needed words to help?"

"No, not always." I rolled my shoulders back and pulled the hovering cupid closer. "But if you need me to say them, then I will," I granted through gritted teeth.

Composing quickly in my mind, I cast my rhyme. *"So Skeeter's chances don't wane or wither, help me find where he placed his quiver. Let's not make the search too narrow, we also need the bow and arrow."*

Making sure the cupid was satisfied, I shut both eyes and concentrated. Images flashed in my head, and I felt the connection to the items draw me to them. His house. The Harvest Moon Cafe. The post office. Images of places where Skeeter might have visited appeared and vanished as I mentally followed the trail. One final place popped up, and I had it.

I let go of him. "How much money did you lose?" I accused.

"Lose?" His puffy cheeks reddened. "Don't know what you're talkin' about."

Rolling my eyes, I got straight to the point. "At Lucky's. Guessing you had some money ridin' on a game of darts with the leprechaun. Not exactly a smart plan, considering that the

Rainbow's End is his bar, and luck tends to be on his side." I raised my left eyebrow at the cupid.

Skeeter hung his head. "I took off my equipment so that I could have more arm movement to throw. And you're right, he took most of everything I had with me."

"Well, he's got your stuff, too. But Lucky's good people, and he has it stashed behind his bar, waiting for you to come get it. So you better hurry," I advised. When he wobbled away in the air, he left someone else waiting for me.

A couple of teenage boys smirked and stepped up, elbowing each other and trying to push the other one into talking to me.

"Can I help you?" I asked with suspicion.

The taller of the two got pushed by his friend and stumbled into the table. "Hey. I, uh, need to find something," he stammered. His face reddened while his friend snickered behind his back.

"And what's that?" asked Blythe, joining me at my side, challenging him.

Clearing his throat for courage, the towering teenager pointed at me. "Don't I get to hold her hand first before I say?"

"Depends." I crossed my arms over my chest, looking up at him. "Do you really have something you need to find?"

Despite his friend's chuckles, the boy in front of me lost his nerve and shook his head. "No, ma'am. Not really. He bolted away from the table, and his friend followed close behind, laughing with too much glee.

Blythe glared in their direction. "I may have to tell their mom about their behavior."

"Who's their mom?" I asked, miffed at being called *ma'am*.

"Lina Mosely."

My mouth dropped. "Those are the two Mosely boys? The last time I remember talking to them, they were knee-high to a gnome."

Blythe elbowed me. "Look out. Here comes trouble."

My brother Matt approached with his wife following behind. "We come in peace," he declared, placing a plate full of food and another cup of sweet tea in front of me.

"I've never been so happy to see you," I said in relief. "Whoever assigned me to this table should be fried in hot oil like chicken."

My brother snickered. "Someone definitely has a sick sense of humor."

I left my post and maneuvered around the table to hug my sister-in-law. Her growing belly pushed against me so that my hug became a little awkward. "Hey, Traci Jo, what do you know? Although I should say Traci Jo and Junior now.

Despite my troubles at the Founders' ceremony, my brother had found the time to celebrate the event and take advantage of the massive amounts of magic released that evening, resulting in our newest family member still cooking inside TJ's belly, which had finally popped out. "I can't wait to meet the new Goodwin."

TJ blushed. "We still have a while to go. In the meantime, tell your brother that he doesn't have to act as my bodyguard for the next few months." Their large dog, Ross, leaned his massive body against my brother, proving he had what it took to take care of his Mistress and the precious cargo she carried.

"See, even Ross the Hoss agrees with your wife." The dog rightfully earned his nickname. If I were a few years younger and a lot of pounds lighter, I might have attempted to ride him like a horse. Instead, I accepted loads of his slobber while trying to pet him. "Are you neglecting your warden duties, Deputy Goodwin?" I nagged.

"No, I do my job just fine." My brother snatched a slice of cornbread from my plate and ate it out of spite. "But tell my stubborn wife that she can hire people to help her take care of the animals. She doesn't have to do it all on her own."

"I keep telling you, pregnancy does not make me an invalid," countered my sister-in-law.

"Still, you shouldn't be moving heavy bags of feed or putting yourself in a dangerous position when you're checking on the larger animals." My brother turned his attention to me. "The Tanners' old mule almost kicked her when she checked on it the other day."

"And yet, I'm still standing." TJ stole the last of the cornbread out of my brother's hand and gulped it down.

I held up my hands. "If you think I'm getting in the middle of this, then the two of you have unicorn manure between your ears. You're both right, and you both love each other. If you start from there, then I'll bet you can figure it out. If you don't, Nana is bound to find out, and then you'll both be sorry."

Reminding my brother about what happened when our grandmother got involved to solve arguments straightened him up real quick. He sighed and kissed his wife on the forehead, the nose, and then her lips. "Let's leave my brat of a sister alone to work the table. Maybe she can spend the rest of her time here pondering whose idea it was to put her there." He flinched away from my swinging hand and ushered TJ from my table with a protective arm hovering behind her.

"Coward," I screamed after him. "Using your pregnant wife as a shield against a hex." Shaking my head, I returned to my seat.

Blythe patted my back and stood up. "I'm gonna go find Lily and Lavender and see if they sold out of all their flowers. I might buy Granny a bunch to brighten her day."

"You mean you really do have a heart beating somewhere in that chest of yours?" I teased, grinning at my friend's sweet soul she did her best to hide from the rest of the world.

"Shh. Don't go spreading that around. I have my reputation to preserve. Hey, you're going to the candidate speeches tonight, right?" she asked as she backed away.

"I intend to. Save me a seat?" I requested.

Shooting me two thumbs up, she waved and headed in the opposite direction. She stopped for a moment to speak to Horatio who handed her a piece of paper.

Maggie West, Sheriff Big Willie's wife, approached me and asked for my help in locating their half-sasquatch baby's favorite blanket. I held up my forefinger and let the little hairy fingers of the baby curl around it. With little effort, the connection formed, and I told her to retrace her steps to the vegetable stand and check on the ground beside a large basket of zucchini. She thanked me and went to retrieve the dropped item.

"Excuse me," croaked a familiar elderly witch who had waited patiently. She squinted at me. "I seem to have misplaced my glasses somewhere."

"Okay, Ms. Flossy. Let me see if I can help." I held out my hand.

When I focused my talents, a clear image formed in my head. My eyes popped open, and I shivered in disgust. "On a bedside table," I uttered. "Do I need to say where?"

Ms. Flossy tittered. "Oh, that's right. I'll have to get Beau to bring them to me." She thanked me and shuffled off.

I would have to scrub my brain at the thought of her being with my roommate. And I might have to threaten the old vampire within an inch of his undead life about bringing his dates back to *my* house. No need to know about any hankyin' or pankyin' happening under my roof when nothing more than a brief friendly hug was going on in my life.

The Mosely boys returned and looked like they were about to try again when they caught sight of Horatio barreling in the direction of the table. The two teenagers scattered, and I greeted the troll with the warmest of hugs. "I'm so happy to see you, Horatio."

"Greetings and salutations, my friend. Are you now

offering your services for a fee? I think that would be a most capital idea." He clapped me on the back, and all the air in my lungs whooshed out.

It took me a second to regain my composure. "No, no money. Just helping."

"If ever you are in need of assistance, I humbly offer my services in helping you research the best way to go about setting up a business." He bowed his head, his scraggly hair falling over his protruding brow. When he straightened, he handed me a piece of paper he'd been holding. "Here."

At the top, it read, "Vote for Juniper, and let every voice—even the smallest one—be heard!" Underneath the slogan that had been carefully handwritten in neat calligraphy letters, somebody had listed out reasons to elect the fairy.

I read the entire list, impressed with each clear and concise point. "Horatio, I would think that since you're one of the candidates that you would be supporting...well...*you*. Not Juniper."

"Alas, my beloved does not possess quite the flair for addressing others. I volunteered to assist her because I would like her to have every possible chance in the world," the troll gushed.

"Thanks, Horatio," a high-pitched voice squeaked. Juniper flew to his side and planted a kiss on his giant cheek. "I'm a bit nervous, but Horatio is right. If I want my issues to be taken seriously, then I need to speak up."

I nodded in full agreement, ignoring the doubt that

anyone would be able to hear her. "I wish you both a whole lot of luck. I'll be rootin' for you tonight at the speeches."

At that word, Juniper shivered, and blue-green fairy dust scattered to the ground. "If I can calm my nerves and get past tonight, then I might just make it."

"Stop your worrying. You will do magnificently. Remember, there is no failure when you succeed at trying." He lifted a large finger and tipped her bitty nose with it with such gentleness that it melted my heart.

"Is that another quote from Shakespeare?" I asked.

"No," the troll winked. "That is all pure Horatio."

The mismatched but perfect couple left me to go practice. The shy fairy had flourished under the attention of her troll, and with support like that, she'd found her bravery. If I had someone like that who could make me blossom, what might I be able to accomplish?

When the Mosely boys returned one last time, I ripped the sign off the table. I didn't need anyone's support to know that today's volunteering of my talents had come to an abrupt end since I'd found the resolve to tell those two troublemakers that they better get lost or risk getting hexed on their adolescent behinds. Bless their hearts.

Chapter Two

The cool breeze cut through the lingering humidity of the day, creating a bearable atmosphere for tonight's event. Musical notes from the efforts of our school band danced in the air and grew louder and more in tune as my feet brought me closer to the park. Never one to be early, I found the area in front of the gazebo packed. All of the chairs were already filled, and unless my friends had reserved me a seat, I would be listening to the speeches from the standing area in the back.

I scanned the crowd for my gang, and my heart warmed when I spotted my girls. None of them had arrived in time to grab a place to sit down, and they beckoned for me to join them standing a few feet behind the last row. After hugging, we girls got down to the important issues at hand.

"Have you seen that hot looking specimen who's new to town?" asked Lavender.

"He's visited the cafe a few times. I don't normally say things like this, but frosted fairy wings, he could make a tick on the back of a dog's neck burst into flames from his looks," Blythe admitted.

"Eww, that's so gross," Alison Kate said, scrunching her nose. "But I have to admit, he is pretty cute."

"Hey, what am I? A big steamin' pile of unicorn dung?" Lee looked less than happy at his new girlfriend's gushing.

Alison Kate cuddled him close and peppered kisses on his cheek. "It's just girl talk, honey bunny. You know you're my shnooky wookums." She rubbed her head into his neck, repeating more syrupy sweet names.

My stomach turned over. "I think I'm going into sugar shock. Holy unicorn horn, you two need to rein in the public display of affection."

Lavender pouted. "Aww, but they are so super cute, and we've been waiting so long for them to get together. Their auras look so bubbly and pink, I can't contain myself." She vibrated in pure joy, earning a stern look from her cousin.

"We may have been wanting them to get together, Lav, but Charli's right. Keep your sugary sweets at the bakery, Ali Kat." Lily crossed her arms over her chest.

Lavender clicked her tongue. "Don't try to play as if you and Ben don't share a similar color surrounding you, Lilypad." Lavender wiggled her finger to indicate the airspace around

Ben and her cousin. "You two may not show it to others, but your relationship is as plain as day to me."

The two cousins squabbled with each other while the rest of us looked on in amazement. Blythe bumped me with her shoulder and pointed. "Remind me never to get that entangled with a man. They're nice to look at, but it will be a hot day in Honeysuckle before I turn into a fool."

"I thought you said there was a new guy to drool at in town?" I accused.

"A girl can look all she wants. And he is seriously drool-worthy." She puckered her lips and whistled.

The hairs on the back of my neck stood up, and a warm tingle rushed down my skin. A strong presence joined me at my right side, and a warm hand brushed my arm. "You ladies are gonna make me blush, talking like that about me," rumbled a deep voice that had become a familiar fixture in my life.

"Good evening, Mr. Channing. I thought you weren't coming to the speeches tonight. Changed your mind?" I teased.

Dash grunted. "I just think that elections don't make any sense. It gives the illusion of freedom, but I guarantee that there's always something lurking behind the scenes. Someone influencing things to get the outcome they want."

"I guess that's not how pack politics work, is it?" I asked. The wolf shifter hardly ever talked about his past, and I ventured to swim into shark-infested waters asking him anything about it.

His eyes flashed amber for a second. "No. That's not how a pack works." Without saying another word, he ended my line of inquiry.

A brief awkward silence followed, and I needed to extract myself to regain my composure and give my cheeks time to stop flaming. "I'm going to go find Flint to wish him good luck." I wove my way through the crowd with quick feet. Walking around the edges, I made it to the back of the gazebo where the candidates gathered.

Following a string of sneezes, I found Flint fumbling with some index cards that looked huge in the gnome's trembling hands. His wife, Gossamer, flitted above him, her fairy wings dusting him in pink.

Flint sneezed again. "Trembling toadstools, Goss, you have to stop hovering over me. I've got this." He squinted at his cards.

"I know, Flinty, dear. I'm just so nervous." More pink dust floated down and covered her husband's beard until the gnome sneezed it off.

"Anything I can do to help?" I called out, hoping to distract my fairy friend.

Goss turned her attention to me and left her husband's side. "Oh, Charli. Do you think things will go okay? My Flinty's been practicing for over a week now, and there's still so much to say." She bit her lip, and her wings flapped in distress.

Flint caught my eye and nodded in thanks for helping his wife. I reassured my friend. "Everything will work out as it should, Goss. You need to stop working yourself into a tizzy. And tonight's about introductions, not to stuff every little thing into one speech. You know your husband is well-liked in the community. I don't think it's possible for him to fail no matter what the outcome is." In my opinion, the gnome was the one to beat in the election.

Horatio and Juniper waved at me, and I responded in kind. Gossamer turned and also wished them good luck from afar. "You supporting everybody, Charli?" she asked through her grin.

Oh, frosted fairy wings. The awkwardness. "Frankly, I'm for anyone to take the new position as long as they have the town's best interests at heart," I dodged. Perhaps I should run for office with my artful deflection skills.

"You mean everybody but Raif, right?" she clarified.

The crowd standing around the lanky vampire was impressive. Unlike the others, Raif looked every bit like a real candidate with advisors at his side. The fact that two of them, Aunt Nora and Hollis Hawthorne, had existing seats on the town council didn't sit well with me. Nana had worked hard at trying to keep herself as neutral as possible since she sat in the high seat of power. But those two shamelessly whispered advice in the vampire's ear. No telling what might happen if Raif earned the new council seat in the election.

"No, I definitely don't support *all* of the candidates." The music from the school's band stopped, and someone announced for everyone to take their seats. "I'd better go join the gang." Waving at all my friends, I excused myself.

A cold hand grabbed my arm and hindered my attempt to leave. "Charlotte. I'm surprised to see you back here. Are you intending to throw your hat in the ring?" My aunt's puckered face mirrored my internal annoyance.

I forced my lips into a smile. "No, Aunt Nora. Just showing my support to those who deserve it."

She released me with a wry grin. "All your good wishes will be wasted once they lose."

After Uncle Tipper's death, my aunt had stayed away from me, and I counted her absence as a blessing. My mother's sister still held no fondness for me—an emotion we both shared. I needed to evacuate before I found a proverbial knife sticking out of my back. Turning on my heel with speed, I ran into a solid mass in front of me.

"My deepest apologies, miss." The impeccable British accent caught me off guard.

"Sorry, Raif," I spit out without looking. When my eyes met the curious gaze looking down on me, I startled. "Oh." My brain scrambled to find other words but failed in their quest.

"And who is this fetching young creature?" the stranger asked. "A fellow campaign manager?"

Raif turned his attention to me and wrinkled his nose. "She is no one of note." The snotty vampire sniffed, dismissing my presence. "She is an interloper who needs to find her place." He pointed to the front of the gazebo, indicating for me to join the rest of the town, but I didn't miss his underlying meaning.

"That's a shame," the stranger said. He grinned, his fangs poking over his lips. "I would enjoy a tête-à-tête with you. In a professional capacity, of course."

I studied the attractive countenance in front of me far longer than I should. Something nagged at the back of my mind, and I attempted to grab onto a faded memory.

Hollis Hawthorne cleared his throat. "Time for you to go, Miss Goodwin." The struggling thought disappeared like smoke, and I shook it off and nodded, too distracted to come up with a witty response.

Making my way to my friends, I stood at the back of the crowd while my grandmother received whoops and hollers along with loud applause as she approached center stage.

"Good evening, y'all," she cried out. "Thank you for coming to tonight's event. This is a landmark occasion for Honeysuckle Hollow. And I know that it comes with great sacrifice on y'all's part to accept that we as a community are changing." She launched into a small speech that I'd heard her rehearse at her house several times.

Dash leaned over to whisper in my ear, his beard tickling my neck. "What's wrong with you?"

"Nothing," I said, unwilling to share my confusion and distraction.

"Sure," he whispered back. "I'll let you have your fib for now."

I shot him a sideways glance, quirking my eyebrow at him. How did he always know?

Shifter, he mouthed, poking his chest with his forefinger.

Whenever I questioned how he knew anything, he always answered the same. Whether or not the animal in him could sense my lie was irrelevant. He liked to remind me that he was more than a man. I never knew if he did it in teasing, flirting, or in warning.

He elbowed me and pointed at the stage. My grandmother introduced Juniper, and the small fairy reluctantly hovered beside Horatio. Her wide eyes gave away her fear, and I wondered if she'd make it through tonight.

Horatio stood up, his head bending down to whisper something in the fairy's ear. I smiled, glad to see their connection. Their match had become fodder for town gossip not long after they'd met at Skeeter's singles event. But neither cared, having found someone else to cling to.

After an awkward pause, Juniper drifted to the middle of the stage. Loud squeaks and squeals erupted from a small group of floating beings behind us. Juniper's employees from her business, Fairy Dust & Clean, screeched their support for their boss. The dour-faced fairy that floated next to them, Moss, barely cracked a smile, staying quiet and contemplative rather than joining her fellow workers in their excitement.

The entire crowd held its breath as the small fairy attempted to speak. Someone shouted, "Speak up," and the diminutive figure shivered, her blue-green dust scattering about her.

"M-m-my name is J-J-J-Juniper. I own the F-F-F-Fairy Dust & C-C-C-clean Services, and I'm running for the n-n-n-new t-t-t-town c-c-c-council s-s-s-seat." Her stuttering increased, and my discomfort for her grew. The fairy clasped her hands in front of her, and I feared she might explode in a ball of anxiety and blue-green dust.

Blythe leaned in on my left side. "Why in the world is she putting herself through this?"

"I have no idea," I said. "I think Horatio encouraged her." All I wanted to do was run up on stage and give the poor thing a hug.

Nana stood up and approached the flailing being. My grandmother's presence filled me with relief. Putting a kind arm around the fairy's waist, she spoke low to Juniper. After she finished, my timid winged friend nodded and cleared her throat.

She stopped trembling and floated with more composure. "M-my name is Juniper, and I am running for the open council seat. I intend to represent everyone in town if I win." A mild level of clapping followed her statement, and the fairy sighed and smiled, gaining a bit of confidence. "But I especially want to give v-voice to those who tend to be ignored or f-forgotten. Everyone must remember that we all choose to live here for different reasons, and we all have the right to an equal s-say."

She paused again, and her employees screamed as loud as they could, the pixies reaching a pitch that made Dash wince. Unfortunately, only a handful of us nearby could hear them. Juniper turned to glance at Horatio who nodded in support. She cleared her throat and finished with a statement she must have rehearsed. "Also, though I may be small, everyone should know that I am strong." She bent her tiny arm and pointed at her nonexistent muscle.

I giggled along with my friends at the fairy's joke. The rest of the crowd chuckled as well, and Juniper left center stage in relief, zipping back to her place with the other candidates, clearly glad her moment in the spotlight was over.

The stage creaked and groaned as the gigantic troll went next. He towered over all of his opponents and the rest of the audience with his massive presence. Pushing the disheveled locks of hair out of his face, he bellowed, thundering loud enough to be heard probably four towns away at least.

"My fellow residents of Honeysuckle, I bid you good evening, and wish you hearty congratulations on this next step in the evolution of our community. As my dear friend Will used to say, *'The web of our life is of a mingled yarn, good and ill together.'* We must heed his wise words and bond as one mighty collective to make our town strong." Horatio launched into an eloquent speech peppered with language that several of the town's residents would have to look up.

It amused me to no end that many of my friends shattered expectations. His intelligence and ability to reason would be an asset to the authority of the town. However, he had a long battle to fight for acceptance. No matter what pretty words flowed out of his mouth, not many people would ever trust a troll.

Horatio continued. "I know that change comes at a cost, one that we are not always willing to pay. However, were I to be so fortunate as to win your hearts and be elected to the seat, I will do my best for every citizen, big or small." He turned his head and smiled at Juniper, who promptly blushed a rosy color closer to Goss's signature hue. "And as we are rational beings, I will also push to broaden our library and its resources. For knowledge remains our best gift. May we use it to make the best choices for our continued future." The troll placed a hand over his heart in sincerity.

The light applause that followed indicated he had lost the crowd. No matter how intelligent he might be, his speech did not win over many people. Still, I beamed at him with pride, happy that he and Juniper had stood up for what they believed in on stage. They were both far braver than me, and I'd lived here almost my entire life.

Dash stiffened at my side. His nostrils flared. "What's that awful stench?"

"What are you talking about?" I murmured under my breath. A few moments later, a sickeningly sweet floral scent filled my nose, and I grimaced.

"Told you," Dash admonished.

I pinched his arm. "Don't let your head shift too big or it'll fill up the entire park."

"That smells like gardenias, right, Lily?" Lavender asked her cousin.

"Gardenias that are on their last legs," Lily agreed, covering her nose.

Ben moaned. "I know of *one* person who wore that scent every day."

Lee took off his glasses and wiped his hand down his face. "I'm having nightmarish flashbacks to primary school."

A commotion at the front of the stage interrupted the evening's proceedings. After much grumbling and shouting, a familiar figure limped its way onto the stage.

"I object," a raspy voice rattled into the air. "We must stop all of this nonsense." The figure waved a thick cane at the audience. My grandmother, along with Aunt Nora and Hollis Hawthorne, rushed into action toward the crooked body interrupting the speeches.

"Who is that?" Dash asked, covering his nose with his hand to block out the smell that had settled over all of us.

"Old Mrs. K," replied most of my gang at the same time.

"Mrs. Kettlefields taught us in primary school. Loved to hear the sound of her own voice droning on and on," added Ben.

"Beat you with a ruler if that voice put you to sleep," said Lee, rubbing the back of his hand in memory.

"That's because you snored," teased Alison Kate.

The crowd in front of the gazebo stage rumbled in disbelief, and we watched the three council members attempt to remove our former teacher. With more strength than anyone would give her credit for, she pushed them off.

"I will have my say, or I will curse you all," she threatened.

"She wouldn't do that, would she?" Blythe asked, gawking at the spectacle.

"There's no telling how many bats she has in her attic now," I said, tapping my head. "Remember, we all used to think she was a bit touched in the head back in the day. It's been many moons since then."

The old lady, with desperation in her eyes, pleaded with the town. "If we go through with this election, it shall spell our doom."

Chapter Three

"For over two hundred years, our small town has been working just fine. Everybody knew everybody else, and we took care of our own. Now, we've got more people here than you can shake a broom at, and the more we add, the more problems we've been getting. Consider the cause of Tipper Walker's death. Was it one of our own that caused his demise? No, it wasn't. It was an outsider, and we don't need no outsiders messin' up our community." Mrs. Kettlefields paused and shook her cane to punctuate her point, sweat dripping down her temples, her eyes widening with fevered passion. She clutched her chest, gasping for air, and glanced with suspicion at the people gathering around her on stage.

"That doesn't sound like Mrs. K at all," commented Ben.

"Wasn't she the one who lectured us again and again on the founding of our town?"

Lee chimed in. "Don't think I haven't forgotten that she made you dress up like a girl for the play she'd written about the event." He flashed a mischievous smile at his friend. "You were so pretty."

I rolled my eyes. "Ben has a point. This sounds nothing like her. If ever there was someone with great pride in our town, it was Mrs. K."

"Sounds like she's lost her marbles in Fairyland," Blythe offered.

"And you know what my Meemaw says," Alison Kate added. "A crazy witch is a dangerous witch."

"And one that needs to be contained," I agreed.

No one understood that sentiment more than me. Due to my great-uncle's faculties not being all there, even though some of his problems may have been induced by the potions that Ashton had given him over time, I'd almost perished because of his spellcasting misfire. After the fact, many people commented that Tipper should have had his powers restrained. The way that Aunt Nora and Hollis glared at Mrs. K suggested that either one might conjure up a large butterfly net to capture her at any second.

Dash spoke in a low voice. "So, you would lock up an old woman like that?"

"Not necessarily. But containing her powers might be important if she's lost her senses. Why? What would you do with someone like her in your pack?"

"You don't want to know," the shifter's deep voice rumbled.

"I think I can handle it."

"Remember that after I've told you." The wolf shifter sighed but kept his voice low, leaning his body against mine as he answered my question. "When I was little, we had an old woman who the pack still cared for even though she'd lost her entire family over decades. It takes a long time for shifters to grow old, so there's no telling exactly what her age was. But she got worse and worse every year, shifting out of control and hunting too close to civilians. My mom did her best to try and keep the woman from harming others and herself, but eventually, my father didn't want to put up with her anymore." Dash paused in his story.

Although my gut told me I didn't want the answer, I still asked the question. "What happened to her?"

"My mom stopped our supply runs to the woman...because the need to take care of her ceased to exist." That was all Dash would give me, and I knew he was done sharing. The shifter life that he revealed to me piece by piece both enamored and scared me. Which was probably his ultimate goal to keep me from getting too close.

A couple of people who worked at the retirement home joined my grandmother on stage, surrounding Mrs. K. The former teacher bent her crooked body forward, her eyes darting side to side like a cornered animal.

Her incessant ranting never stopped. "And another thing. This newer generation ain't much better, despite what I taught them. You got the young Lee Chalmers' son messing about with human technology, which has no business mixing with magic in the first place. And then there's Charlotte Goodwin, who's been a handful since she was little, catchin' a death curse and almost dyin'. It's all too much. No more change. We can't handle it."

The group of people closed ranks around her and inched forward with their arms out. A breathless hush fell over the crowd as we waited for the capture of Mrs. K. The old woman straightened up and touched her head in despair, a keening sound bursting from her lips.

My grandmother stopped the others and approached from the side. "Eugenia, why don't you follow me and come get some sweet tea. I think you're overtired and overheated."

The poor woman nodded and followed my grandmother, muttering in confusion and shaking her head.

"Well, who knew an election could be so dramatic? And look at you, getting a personal shout-out." Dash brushed his finger down my arm.

"I don't think anyone expected it to go that way," I said, keeping my eyes forward and trying to ignore the path of flames his touch left behind.

Hollis approached the center of the stage. "Ladies and gentlemen, I thank you for your patience and your kind consideration. I think with a little more effort, we can finish introducing the candidates tonight and get to the desserts that you fine folk have provided. So how about we have a round of applause for those candidates who have already presented?"

Moving aside, Hollis gave way to Flint and let the gnome take center stage. With everyone still shaken from Mrs. K's interruptions, it took a few moments for us to truly hear Flint's speech. But after a quick rundown of his duties in Honeysuckle as a gate guard at our borders, he garnered the attention of most of the citizens.

"If elected, I will continue to strive to keep Honeysuckle the safe haven it has always been for any magical beings that choose to live here. It has done me and mine no end of goodness, and with the new addition to our family, I will strive to make our town the best place for my offspring to grow up in. Thank you."

An entire unicorn could have leaped into my gaping mouth. "Did he just tell us what I think he told us?"

Alison Kate hugged Lee in glee, and Blythe smiled with pure joy. "Pretty sure he just announced that our friend Goss is with child."

"No wonder she was a nervous wreck backstage," I commented. But I had completely missed the clues.

"I guess you can't solve every mystery," joked Dash, poking my rib with his elbow.

The gnome blushed with the cheers of congratulations and waved to the side at his wife who sprinkled pink fairy dust on everyone close to her, tears streaming down her rosy cheeks. I'd have to give her a big squeeze after the last speech.

"Is it over?" asked Dash.

"I wish," I muttered, pointing to Raif approaching the center with grave solemnity.

The vampire spoke in his clipped British accent and delivered a speech that had more polish and finesse than the others' combined. Aunt Nora and Hollis nodded their heads in absolute agreement to every point that Raif stated, especially when he talked about bringing in more people from the outside world and expanding the options of our lives.

On a scale from one to ten, one being Mrs. K's shared rant about change and ten being blowing up the entire town and starting from scratch, Raif landed at a solid seven. His ideas were progressive and controversial, pushing the expectations of most of the town's citizens. But his presentation, his presence, and the clear support he garnered from the other council members would make him a hard opponent to beat. His speech lasted longer than the others, and I grew bored. Alison Kate and Lee excused themselves as they scooted around me.

"I've got to go help Sprinkle and Twinkle set up some of the desserts," she whispered in a low voice.

"You need help? Oh, sure." I volunteered myself to escape, and found the rest of my group, including Dash, heading over to the nearby picnic tables lined with all kinds of sweets and goodies. Raif's voice echoed around us, but we ignored him, helping the two retired tooth fairies arrange the desserts by color rather than type just for fun.

After a generous round of applause for the vampire candidate and some final words from my grandmother, a mass of people rushed toward the tables to stuff their faces. Nana understood that it wasn't their consciences or the rational need to weigh and balance who might be the best candidate to vote for that filled the park. The promise to fill their stomachs with good food would always act as the best motivator.

"I think I'm gonna head out." Dash touched my arm.

I reached up and brushed a smear of frosting from his upper lip and whiskers. "Had enough?"

His eyes burned into me. "I've barely gotten started." He gripped my wrist in his hand and captured my thumb in his mouth, licking the frosting off and grazing my skin with his teeth. Warm tingles shot down to my belly, and I barely contained the shiver that shuddered my body. "I'd be happy to stay and walk you home when you're ready," the shifter offered.

I swallowed hard. "I-I think I might take Nana home. She's had a hard night." Pixie poop. Why did my mouth utter the truth before my brain caught up? Next time a good-looking man asked to escort me home, I needed to say *yes*, no matter what.

"As you wish." Dash winked and left.

"Phew, that man sure is a handful," Blythe said, riling me up.

"More like a mouthful if you ask Charli and her thumb," Lily added, her eyes twinkling at me.

The heat from my cheeks could melt the ice cream on top of my slice of pecan pie. "Shut up."

Lavender opened her mouth to tell everyone what color my aura was, but I held up a hand at her in warning. "Don't you dare."

"I wasn't. I was going to point out that the detective is heading your way. He's been standing there, watching you for a bit." She pointed behind me, and I turned.

Mason strode straight for me, a grimace on his face. Whatever he was working on, it couldn't be good. The prospect of helping him again sent a zing of excitement through me. It had been a long time since he'd asked me for anything, and I was beginning to wonder if he'd forgotten where I lived.

"Detective Clairmont, I didn't know you were here tonight," I joked, using formality to break the chilly distance between us.

"Isn't everybody?" he replied in a stern voice, keeping that wall of ice firmly in place.

"For the most part," I agreed. "Is there something I can help you with?"

"Yes. Follow me." He didn't even meet my gaze when he spoke, and gave me no option to refuse, turning around and stomping back the way he'd come. I followed behind like an obedient puppy, hoping for him to throw me some scraps so I might grab a clue about where the two of us stood.

"Mason, slow down," I cried out.

"Hurry up," he insisted, not lagging for a second. He led the way to an area in between the gazebo stage and the desserts.

A loud British voice chastised some unlucky target. "You are completely useless."

"I'm sorry, Raif," my roommate Beau apologized. He bowed his head in submission to the other vampire.

"Sorry doesn't make up for what you've done." Raif's nose pointed higher in the air than ever.

As I approached, I spotted pink tears forming in Beau's eyes. Nobody talked to my roommate like that, and I broke away from Mason to support my friend. "What's going on?"

"Oh, good. The detective found you." Raif thrust a finger in Beau's face. "This moron lost my precious pug."

Mason joined the fray. "I think the situation requires a sense of calm and not accusations. I'm sure that Charli here can help find your dog."

"I didn't do anything," sniffled Beau. "I held onto the leash as you asked me to. He was by my side throughout the entire event. Except..."

"Except when?" Raif stepped closer to my roommate, seething. "When did my precious baby disappear?"

"There was so much commotion when the speeches were interrupted by Eugenia. And once that was all over, it took me a few minutes to figure out that Sir Barklay had worked his way out of his collar." The pudgy vampire held up the sparkling leather collar attached to a leash.

"Are those real diamonds?" I asked in surprise.

Raif snatched the collar and leash away from Beau. "That's none of your business. I want you to do whatever it is you do to find my sweet boy. Now."

"Whatever is the commotion here?" The man I'd run into before the speeches approached us. "Raif, you look positively pale, and that's saying something about a fellow vampire." He clapped his friend on the back.

"My pug. He's gone," whined Raif.

"Oh, dear. Perhaps we should form a search party. I would be happy to help organize the effort," offered the newcomer.

"That's quite all right." Raif took a slight step away. "The detective here has already enlisted Charlotte's help in finding my Barklay."

The complete change in the snooty vampire's demeanor and speech floored me. Two seconds ago, he was a raving lunatic, distraught and inconsolable. Now he spoke with such deep emotion that I almost felt sorry for him.

"And what is it that Miss Charlotte can do for you?" the fellow vampire asked.

"I find things, Mr.—"

"Mallory. Damien Mallory. Longtime friend of Raif here and his current guest for the time being. I would like to see these talents of yours at work, Miss Charlotte." His focus on me and not his friend's dog perked my interest.

Raif shot me a look of frustration, and my annoyance with him returned. It was too bad that Lady Eveline had chosen this specific time to travel to Europe to visit with friends. Usually, she could appease Raif and ease his moods. But maybe she'd left when she did in order to avoid dealing with him while he ran for the council seat.

If I could refuse him, I would. But I took pity on him for

missing his dog. If anyone had messed with my Peaches, I'd be in a similar state.

With a sigh, I acquiesced. "Here. Give me your hand." I extended mine and waited for the cold touch of the tall vampire.

Raif placed his hand in mine with reluctance, probably wishing he could do anything else but touch someone he deemed less than him.

"Concentrate on what it is you want to find," I instructed.

The vampire candidate closed his eyes and repeated his pug's name over and over.

Concentrating, I gathered my powers and focused them in my center. I waited for an image to present itself. Nothing. Clearing my throat, I whispered under my breath, *"Even though he's awfully smug, help me find his precious pug."*

Still nothing. Not even a thin line of glowing connection. Sweat broke out on my brow, and I opened one eye to find everyone staring at me.

"Did you get anything?" Mason asked.

Shaking my head, I admitted the truth. "No."

Raif snatched his hand out of mine. "I knew it. I knew she wouldn't help me. You think I didn't see you and your friends leave the audience early during my speech? I thought this town was all about politeness, and yet you dare to hold back with me? Not even willing to help when a precious baby is involved."

Damien attempted to console Raif, but his friend shrugged off his embrace. "I think it's premature to accuse young Charlotte of not helping you. Perhaps it will take something more."

"Or maybe he can find his dog on his own," I shot back at him. "I don't hold back, Raif. I'm not the one who discriminates."

My blood boiled, and I debated standing my ground and taking on the insufferable fool or storming off. Mason offered no help in the situation despite my pleading gaze at him. Beau spoke up in my defense, but his low trembling voice couldn't be heard over all the yelling.

My brother approached us, waving his hands. "I think I have something here that belongs to you." He moved to the side and revealed Mrs. Kettlefields standing behind him.

The old woman held the vampire's pug in her arms. "This sweet boy was running around the tables and I caught him. Young Mr. Goodwin here says he belongs to you. But I found him and he has no collar." She grasped the pooch with firm hands, the little dog whimpering at her touch.

"That's my sweetums," insisted Raif. He stormed toward the elderly witch and snatched his pet from her hands. "I suppose you took him on purpose. Part of your plan to throw off the election."

I shook my head. "Beau already told you that Barklay disappeared while she was on stage, so she didn't snatch your precious pug. She found him for you, so you better thank her, not accuse her."

"His name is *Sir* Barklay." Raif shut his mouth, refusing to offer any gratitude.

Damien stepped between the two of them. "My dear madam, please allow me to extend my friend's thanks to you for finding his beloved pet." He reached out to touch her arm, and she jumped away from his grasp.

"I'd like to go home now," she insisted to my brother.

"I think that's a good idea, Mrs. Kettlefields." Matt escorted her away.

"You've got your dog back. Y'all have a good night," I offered in a clipped tone. Standing aside, I waited for Mason to say something to me.

He addressed the three vampires instead. "I need to get back to the station. Goodnight, gentlemen." The detective walked off without one glance my way, leaving me behind.

"Goodnight, Detective," I called out.

"Goodnight, Miss Goodwin," he replied without turning around.

I returned to my friends in utter dejection. Not only had my talents not worked at all but also my charms no longer worked with the detective. Not even an extra slice of homemade red velvet cake with thick cream cheese frosting could sweeten the sour taste of failure.

Chapter Four

Something tickled my nose, and I waved my hand to brush it away. The sensation returned, and I tried to smack whatever it was that dared to bother me. When the irritating touch happened a third time, I captured the culprit with my hand.

"Whoever this is, you're dead to me," I declared to the offender.

"If you kill me, then you don't get any ham and jelly biscuits."

I opened one eye and glared at my brother. "Who made them? You?"

He scoffed. "Of course not. I just came from Nana's. I'll make some coffee if you'll shake a tail feather, Birdy."

It'd taken me a long time to fall asleep last night. I replayed over and over again my interaction with Raif, focusing on my inability to make any connection with his dog. Finding a lost animal like that should have been child's play. Literally, I could have done it when I was seven or eight. Why didn't my talents work last night?

By the time I tamed my hair into something presentable, the scent of coffee caught my attention. I stomped my way down the old creaky staircase and plopped down into the wooden chair at the small table in the kitchen, folding forward and leaning my head on the table. My brother slid a mug in front of me. "Here, Birdy."

"Don't call me that," I mumbled into the surface of the table. Lifting my head enough to take a sip of coffee, I savored the warmth of it for two seconds, and then slammed my head back down on the table.

"What has you all out of sorts?" my brother asked.

My absolute abject failure, I thought. "Nothing," I replied.

Without looking up, I snatched a biscuit from the plate in the center of the table. Once again, I lifted my head enough to take a bite and another swallow of coffee before dropping it down again on the cool surface.

"Gee. I completely believe you," Matt teased.

"It's nothing," I managed with a mouthful of biscuit, ham, and jelly. Even one of my favorite breakfast items couldn't lift my spirits this morning.

"Say it, don't spray it." He wiped off his face. "At least don't waste Nana's buttermilk biscuits."

"What are you doing here anyway?" I asked, sitting up and accepting the plate he pushed at me.

"TJ is out with the horses," Matt said. He and my sister-in-law had fixed up an old barn on part of Tipper's land, which now belonged to my brother. The house and some of the property around it belonged to me, but he owned the rest thanks to our generous great-uncle and his will.

However, Matt had still asked for my blessing before fixing up the old barn to TJ's standards in order to house a few rescue horses. My sister-in-law had a soft spot for the large animals, and it frustrated her that her pregnancy would affect her ability to ride.

"I can't believe you're in here while she's out there scooping the poop all by herself," I accused.

"I'm making her?" my brother exclaimed in frustration. "I tried to tell her we could hire someone to help, and she nearly bit my head off. Asked me if I was saying that she was weak or something. Which is nothing like what I said."

I failed at stifling a giggle. "So what you're saying is that you're hiding out in here."

"No. I brought my little sister some breakfast."

"Coward."

"Husband of a crazy pregnant woman," Matt replied, pointing at himself.

"It's going to be a lot of fun watching you try to handle things," I chuckled.

He groaned. "You could at least have some sympathy."

"I'm a girl. Any sympathy I have lies with the pregnant woman. Solidarity and sisterhood." I raised my fist in the air.

"You're all crazy," my brother breathed out.

"Say that to her. I dare you. She'll hex your hiney so fast." I continued to give my brother grief until he couldn't take it anymore. Changing the subject to save his sanity, I took another bite of biscuit. "So where did you find Mrs. K last night?"

"The caretakers from the retirement home swear they had left her sitting at a table with a plate of desserts and a cup of iced tea. But she was walking on the edge of the crowd, muttering to herself and holding the dog that turned out to be Raif's. I heard all the commotion where you were and put everything together. When I tried to take the dog away from her, she fought me, so I escorted her to you guys."

Remembering the haunted gaze in her eyes, I shuddered. "Last night was weird, right? I mean, she was always a little cuckoo in her passion about the town's history. But this was on another level."

"You should've heard her, muttering that it wasn't right and that she she wished she could remember. I couldn't make heads or tails of what she was saying, but she was clearly in distress. After we got her to return the dog, I took her back to the retirement home. I hope she settled down after that."

"What did Nana say this morning?" I asked.

"She wants things to settle down a bit, and then maybe visit Mrs. Kettlefields herself. Nana's got her hands full with the election, so I don't want her distracted any more than she has to be." Matt covered his worry with a sip of his drink.

"I think last night went beyond the distraction," I said.

My brother scooted back from the table and stood. He grabbed one more biscuit. "Well, I'm off."

"Going to the station?" I asked.

"No. I'm going to go approach my wife with courage and see if she'll accept my help with the horses." He picked up Peaches who must have been rubbing around his ankles under the table, and placed her orange furry body in my lap.

"Good luck," I wished my brother, holding my kitty in my arms and walking him to the door.

"I'm going to need it," he admitted. He waved at me and walked through the field toward the barn.

"He definitely is," I muttered to Peaches. She squirmed to be let down before bounding outside to chase a dragonfly.

Fortified with another cup of coffee, I charged upstairs and opened the door to another room full of chaos. When my great-uncle left me his house, I knew he meant for it to be a beneficial gift. But his years of hoarding made it a treasure trove of trash that took time to sift through. A normal person might take a shovel to it all without going through every scrap of paper, but beyond the need to straighten up the house, I was looking for something specific.

Somewhere inside, there might be paperwork or clues to my origins. Beau had accidentally revealed to me that Tipper had something to do with my adoption. I wanted proof of the truth of that statement, not because I doubted my pudgy vampire roommate but because a part of me desired to know more than just my life in Honeysuckle.

Sure, my family was my family. My brother was my

brother. That would never change. But if I had a clue to follow in finding the biological family that I came from, then maybe I could understand my powers. Or at least have someone to ask what to do when they completely failed.

After a couple of hours spent up to my elbows in useless trash, I sat on my behind in full-on depressed mode. I'd barely made a dent with my efforts in one room. When Beau was home, he helped bolster my spirits, promising that maybe the next piece of paper I picked up might be the one. But without him here, the reality that my life was drowning in a sea of stockpiled trash overwhelmed me.

A sharp knock on the front door startled me out of my dark thoughts. Springing up, I ran downstairs to answer it. When I opened the door, Dash stood on the other side of the screen, his thumbs hooked in his pockets. "Morning, ma'am."

I grinned from ear to ear, unable to hide my joy and relief at his presence. "Mornin' yourself. You want to come in? I think there's at least one last ham and jelly biscuit left."

The wolf shifter shook his head. "No, I'm good in the food department. But I would like to request your presence out here for a moment."

I pulled the door wide and joined him on the porch. "What have you got up your sleeves?" I asked.

"Not wearing any sleeves," he replied, showing off his muscular arms and bulging biceps. "What you see is what you get."

"I wish," I muttered under my breath as I walked down the porch steps.

Two bikes sat in front of the house. Dash walked around and presented the first one to me with a flourish of his hands. "Ta-da," he sang out.

"That's my bike," I admitted.

"Yes, it is."

"But you already gifted that to me before," I said in confusion.

Dash held up a finger. "But now it's the new and improved bike. I got Lee to work his magic on it. He said he spellcrafted it so that it will move on its own."

His childish glee tickled me. "A motorized bicycle?"

"I wouldn't call it a motorcycle."

"Like mine, you know, the one you're supposed to have fixed for me?" I needled him.

"I'm still waiting on parts for Old Joe. But in the meantime, would you like to take a trip into town with me and try her out?" He wiggled his eyebrows and beckoned me forward with a finger.

"Give me just a second." Disappearing into the house, I ran upstairs to get myself into better shape. I'd never been a girly-girl type to worry about or fuss over her looks, but something made me want to appear more than just presentable.

I brushed my teeth and pulled back my hair into a ponytail. With a final glance into the mirror, I approved my appearance and ran back downstairs. Voices coming from the porch welcomed me.

Joining them, I found Dash speaking with my roommate.

"Beau, you didn't come home last night," I commented.

"After what happened with Raif, I needed a little TLC time. And since you have a strict rule about me bringing my lady friends back to the house, I decided to spend my time at the retirement home."

I managed not to grimace at the implications of my roommate's night dalliances, but Dash failed at hiding his surprise. "You wooing the ladies there?" he asked.

"From time to time," admitted my vampire roommate. "Last night, I spent an hour or two with Cordelia Jenkins. A perfectly lovely woman, although we were interrupted by a commotion. The same poor soul who found Raif's dog had a bit of a breakdown."

"She did?" I asked.

Beau nodded. "She became very agitated, crying out odd accusations about somebody making her say the things that she did on stage. They had to bring Dr. Andrews in to calm her down." The pudgy vampire leaned closer to us and lowered his voice. "The rumor going around the home this morning was that they're talking about enacting a binding."

"No," I uttered in absolute disbelief. "It's been an age since they've done that. But if she's so out of control, then she can be a danger to herself and those around her," I admitted. Still, the thought of having anyone's magic stripped from them made me go cold all over.

"Sounds like a lot of trouble," Dash said.

I frowned at him. "It's how we take care of our own," I

responded, trying to keep the thoughts of the power of his pack life at bay.

"I left before any other drama happened this morning. I think I will take a much-deserved nap." Beau yawned and opened the screen door. "You two kids have fun."

"Shall we?" Dash gestured at the bikes.

A ride was exactly what I needed to clear my head. I raced him down the steps and straddled the bicycle. "Show me how the new-fangled magic works."

The wolf shifter gave me an explanation about the switch on the side of the gearshift. I could either ride it like normal or turn the switch on, which would activate the spell.

Dash did his best to explain how the magic worked but got more and more frustrated as I asked questions. "I don't know," he exclaimed. "You just turn it on, magic happens, and the bike goes."

I knew my friend Lee had a particular talent in spellworking his magic with technology and objects. No doubt he had given explicit instructions to Dash that were hard for anyone else to understand.

"No worries," I said. "Let's take them out to the road and see what happens."

We walked the bikes side-by-side through the field until we reached pavement. "You ready?" Dash mounted his bicycle.

"As I'll ever be," I exclaimed. Flipping on the switch, I recognized the initial dizzying rush of power over the object and my body. I took off at a faster pace than I could set with my own legs.

"Hey, that's not fair," called out Dash from behind.

A carefree giggle bubbled out of me. "Last one to town buys lunch." I left him in the dust as the wind whipped around me. Letting out a loud whoop, I leaned forward and urged the bike on.

❧

"YOU CHEATED," accused Dash as he pulled up beside me on Main Street.

"I'm hearin' a whole lot of whinin' and not seein' a whole lot of payin' up," I teased. "Shall we go to the cafe?"

We parked our bikes and wandered down the sidewalk.

"Next time, I want a fair contest. Plus, we never shook on any bet, so I don't see why I have to buy you food." Lifting his top lip, he fake growled in complaint.

"I suppose that's true," I admitted.

"But I'm happy to buy you lunch anyway." He bumped me with his hip. "Loser."

"Are you looking at your reflection in the window?" I asked, bumping him back. "Because if I recall, I got to town first."

"Hey, is that your friend waving at you over there?" Dash asked.

"Nice try, but you're not distracting me," I insisted.

He stopped walking. "No, over there," he pointed.

I stopped talking and looked in that direction. Horatio was gesticulating wildly with his arms. "Charli," he called out, his loud voice echoing off the storefronts. "If you could, I request your presence with immediate haste."

I rushed over to the troll, Dash following close behind. "What's wrong, Horatio?"

"I...I..." Horatio stammered. "Forgive me, but it is not something I can tell you outright. The situation is more something you have to see." He glanced around in fear. "Come inside with me," he insisted.

The troll took wide strides up the stairs and disappeared into the library. Dash looked at me, his face full of warning, but curiosity got the better of me. I followed close behind, and the wolf shifter stayed glued to my side.

The unmistakable smell of old books filled my nostrils. In its heyday, the building had been bustling with people checking out books and children reading inside in hidden corners. It had fallen under neglect over the years and seemed more dingy than inviting.

"Something's not right." Dash's eyes flashed amber. "I smell death."

"I think that's the scent of old books," I countered, speaking in a hushed tone. Even though the building was empty, I still felt the need to whisper.

"No," said Horatio. "Your friend here is correct. Look." He ushered us to the tall stacks of books, stopping and giving us time to spot the object that didn't belong. In the middle of the row, sheltered between full bookshelves lay a body.

The sickeningly sweet scent of gardenia hit my nose at the same time the funk of decay did. My stomach turned, and my hand flew to my mouth to guard against anything coming out.

"Don't tell me that's—" started Dash.

"It is," I managed. "It's Mrs. Kettlefields."

Chapter Five

The dead body rested in a contorted fashion, her eyes open and filmed over in that deceased kind of way.

"We need to get a warden here," I exclaimed.

"Yeah, why did you bring Charli in instead of one of them?" Dash asked.

Horatio blew out a breath. "I do not know. I must confess, when I walked outside, I was in a quandary as to what action to take. You must understand that my first thoughts were that it looks suspicious that her body was found in the library, the one place where I have been allowed to have full reign and control. You cannot deny that this town has had its issues with my presence before."

"But why me?" I asked, unable to stop staring at the poor woman.

"Because you have a knack for finding things. And, forgive my impertinence, but I thought that your presence on Main Street was fortuitous at that exact moment." The troll wiped his mighty hands down his protruded brow and face.

I touched his arm in sympathy. "I get it, but we really do need to bring the wardens in on this. If we don't, then the suspicion will lay on you even more."

Horatio hung his head. "But, of course, you are in the right."

Dash tugged on my arm. "Let's go, Charli."

I shook my head. "No. You go. I want to stay and take a closer look."

"Charli," insisted the shifter. "You don't need to do that. It's not your job."

I looked at him and the troll. "I don't have to, but I want to. See if you can find my brother, although it may be faster to go straight to the warden station."

Dash blew out a frustrated breath. "Fine. You can stay here until I bring a warden back with me. Then you leave."

I didn't appreciate his demanding tone. "Then I'll make up my own mind and my own decision at that point." A small part of me hoped that maybe the wardens would request my help in figuring out what had happened to my old teacher. "Now, go."

"Yes, ma'am," Dash replied, all trace of flirting gone from his response.

Left behind, I returned to the matter at hand. With careful steps, I walked around the disheveled body. I mentally took notes on as many details as possible, saying them out loud in order to cement them in my head. "Did you find a cane anywhere near here?" I asked.

"No," replied Horatio. "Why?"

"She needed one to get around. When she waved it on stage, she would lose her balance. No cane means she didn't come here under her own power."

"Nicely observed," said Horatio. "What else?"

"She's dressed in a nightgown. Clearly, that adds to my suspicion she was brought here rather than making the journey on her own."

"She might have been sleepwalking," offered the troll.

"It's possible," I conceded. "However, I've never known the woman to step out into society without being appropriately clothed. Look at her neck."

The troll leaned over the body as best he could. "I don't see anything."

I pointed at some purple marks on her pale skin. "That looks like bruising to me."

"Somebody put their hands around her neck. Poor woman," lamented the troll.

My eyes roamed over the dead woman's body, looking for any other noticeable clues. I avoided going above the neck because I wasn't sure if I'd be able to handle looking into her open eyes again. Yes, I wanted to help, but knowing the victim might render me useless.

The unnatural bend of her body more than suggested that she didn't fall on her own. "Somebody definitely laid her here." I crouched down to look at the soles of her feet. "See? No dirt."

"So she was placed here on purpose." Horatio frowned.

"Looks like it." The stench of her perfume and the mortification of her body overwhelmed my senses. I closed my eyes and covered my nose with my hand.

"Here." Horatio handed me a handkerchief. Instead of using it to block out the smell, I thanked him and used the fabric to pick up her lifeless hand. "See here? She has blood on her fingertips and under her fingernails."

"And I think we can take it from here, Miss Goodwin," called out a familiar voice. Mason rounded the corner. "I'll ask you to let go of the body and back away."

I placed Mrs. K's hand down with gentle intent and held up my own, showing the detective the handkerchief. "I didn't touch her with my bare hands."

"You shouldn't be touching her at all," admonished Mason. "As I said, we can take it from here. And you," he turned his attention to the troll. "It was you who found her?"

"I did." Horatio looked at the body and back at the detective. "I feel most bereft for the poor lady."

"I'm sure," muttered Mason, taking out his notebook from his pocket. "And when did you find her?"

"When I came in to open the library this morning. Ten o'clock, I believe, Detective," answered my friend.

Mason glanced at his watch. "It's almost lunchtime. Why have we been brought in now?"

"I will admit, I did not discover her right away. It took the re-shelving of a few books for me to stumble upon her."

"And so the first person you contacted was Charli and not a warden." The detective's point came out as a statement rather than a question.

"I did not search specifically for her, Detective Clairmont. However, when I exited the library initially, I found her within the area. For whatever reason, I asked her to verify who the lady is. Was, I mean," stumbled Horatio.

Mason instructed both of us to step away from the body to give the other wardens a chance to do their job, peppering us with more questions. With each one, it became clear whom the detective suspected.

"Horatio didn't do it, Mason, if that's what you're trying to imply," I protested.

"And what makes you the expert in this? Were you with Horatio so that you can vouch for him?" His professional gaze chilled me.

"No. But there is nothing to suggest that he did do it other than she was found in the library," I pointed out.

"By him," said Mason. "And he did not alert us to her presence right away, which calls him into suspicion at least."

"And while you're asking him questions, you're not the one taking notice of the important things," I insisted.

"Like what?" Mason asked.

I filled him in on my observations. The detective listened and wrote things down in his notebook. "Thank you for doing a job that doesn't belong to you, but I must insist that you leave now. And Horatio, I would like you to accompany me to the station." He turned his back to us and ordered the other wardens to get the body onto a nearby stretcher.

With a warden on either side of the body, they used their magic to lift her into the air. When she settled on the stretcher, her head lolled to the side in my direction. Her empty, glassy eyes stared at me while her mouth gaped in horror as if still trying to draw in a final breath.

"Wait a minute," I called out.

Mason rushed to me. "Charli," he hissed. "That's enough. I don't need you here, and I don't need your help."

His words stung, but I brushed them off. "No, I mean, look at her mouth." Something white was sitting in her open jaws.

"Tweezers," commanded Mason. "Does anybody have any tweezers?"

"Horatio, grab me two pencils," I ordered.

"Don't move," countered Mason. "Here, you two. Give me your pencils." The nearby wardens handed over their writing implements.

Holding them in my hand like a pair of chopsticks, I approached the body. With care, I clasped the white object between the tips of the two pencils and pulled on it gently. It came out and fell, a line of sticky saliva snapping away as it hit the floor.

Mason gestured his hands at the object, and it lifted in the air. With a few twists of his wrists and a flourish of his fingers, the article unfolded and grew larger, revealing a wrinkled piece of paper. "There's something written on it," the detective said.

I edged closer to it. "Looks like a poem." I read the lines out loud.

"Turn, turn, my wheel! All things must change
To something new, to something strange;
Nothing that is can pause or stay;
The moon will wax, the moon will wane,
The mist and cloud will turn to rain,
The rain to mist and cloud again,
To-morrow be to-day."

"I know those words," declared Horatio. He broke the command of the detective and ran off with heavy stomps. When the troll returned out of breath, he held out a book in his hand. "It's Henry Wadsworth Longfellow." He opened the hardback to reveal the torn page. "I believe it came from here."

"I'll take that." Mason gave orders for a warden to bag the book. He made another flourish with his hands, and a shimmering protection layered over the book and sealed it. He took it from the troll, handing it off to one of the other wardens, and issued orders for them to take the body out the back of the library instead of out the front door onto Main Street.

Mason turned his attention back to the two of us. "I'm going to lock this place down under warden protection. You, you're coming with me," he directed at Horatio. "Charli, you need to go home."

"But don't you want my help?" I asked. "Perhaps there's something I can track down?"

Mason escorted me to the front door. "If there's something to find, then I might be in contact with you. Until then, let me do my job."

I pulled on his arm to stop him. "Mason, what's going on?" More questions popped into my head, but I focused on the one that mattered. "Did I do something wrong?"

"No, Charli. It's not you who did something wrong." He cast his eyes down and scratched the back of his head.

"I don't understand. That implies that you think *you* did something, and for the life of me, I can't think of anything." I wanted to shake him out of whatever mood affected him.

Without another glance at me, Mason opened the door. "Let me handle things my way for once. Please."

The sun hurt my eyes. Already a crowd had gathered on the front steps of the library. Linsey forced her way through the crowd and confronted Mason. "I heard you found a body. Care to elaborate?"

"No comment," replied Mason.

Lily's younger sister turned her attention to me. "How about you? Are you involved in another murder, Charli?"

Back off, Linsey," I grated through my clenched teeth. "Or I will hex your hiney."

"So, that's not a no?" challenged the annoying reporter wannabe.

"Miss Goodwin was assisting me inside. And that is all you need to know. Good day," Mason dismissed her.

Inquisitive eyes burrowed into me, and I needed a quick getaway. A shrill whistle snapped me to attention. I ran in its direction and found Dash around the corner. He stood shirtless beside the two bikes, sweat dripping down his muscled torso. Pulling his shirt over his head, he covered his muscled skin.

"Were you naked?" I asked.

"How else do you think I got to the warden station so fast? I don't shift with my clothes still on." The corner of his mouth lifted in amusement.

People started heading our way to ask more questions. I straddled the bike and flipped the switch. "Let's get out of here."

We took off down the street, leaving the rest behind. About halfway back to my house, I turned the switch off, wanting to burn some energy with the power of my own muscles. My mind raced through the details I had noticed. Mason's treatment of Horatio and me repeated over and over again, and I grew angrier at each mental replay. I stopped the bike in the middle of an intersection.

"What are you doing?" asked Dash.

"I'm sorry. I've gotta go." Turning my bike in the opposite direction, I headed toward the warden station.

Chapter Six

I arrived at the station and parked my bike, running inside in a huff. When I got to the front desk, I didn't know what to say or why I was there in the first place. I stood in indecision, contemplating whether to stay or go home for too long before someone noticed me.

"Oh, hey, Charli," called out Zeke. "You lookin' for your brother?"

"Not exactly." I panicked, unable to come up with the reason why I was there. "I'm here to speak to Mason. I mean, Detective Clairmont."

"He's busy at the moment, but I don't think he would mind if you wanted to wait." Zeke offered a nearby seat.

"Thanks," I uttered. Sitting down, I did my best to be patient. But I couldn't stop the replay in my head, and I found myself more steamed than before. By the time Mason's deep tone echoed down the hall, I was in tune with it and ready to go on the attack. However, he escorted Horatio out, and I wanted a chance to talk to my friend.

"Charli," Mason said in a calm voice. "Why am I not surprised? You have a habit of not taking my advice."

"I want to talk to you in a second," I demanded. But first, I took the troll by the hand and pulled him outside. "Tell me," I insisted. "What did they say or do?"

Horatio reassured me. "I am not under arrest, if that is your concern. I have, however, been informed not to leave Honeysuckle anytime soon, which is not an imposition due to the fact of my involvement in the election. So it shall not change my future plans more than to add grief and concern to my life. I do not believe that they have any idea who might have brought harm to the old woman."

"As long as they follow the evidence that points away from you, then I'm okay with that," I exclaimed.

"That's the problem, my dear. Your detective is acting under the philosophy of Occam's razor. The simplest explanation is usually the best. If I were him, then I would suspect me as well. She was found in the library, which is my domain. If you are right and she was choked to death, it would not be an unreasonable leap to think that a troll with as large of hands as I possess could easily manage her delicate nape."

"What about the poem?" I asked.

Horatio sighed. "My affinity for language and the written word is renowned. Although the American masters are not my forte, it does seem as if somebody is going to extraordinary lengths to have me at the very least be considered a suspect. Whoever they are, they have achieved their goal to great success."

"But the words and their meaning. I think they're talking about change, right?" My mind raced to make sense of it all.

The troll smiled in acknowledgment. "You are indeed correct. The entire poem speaks about how nothing can remain the same."

"If I didn't know better, I would think that it was a political statement," I observed.

"Another pointed arrow aimed in my direction, I think." He rubbed his chin in contemplation.

"It could be for any of the candidates, Horatio. Or meant as a message to anyone who believes that our town shouldn't change at all. But none of those pieces of evidence definitively call you into suspicion." I intended to say exactly that to Mason in a few moments. "And what about the blood under the fingernails? Did the detective say anything about that?"

The troll shook his head and smiled down at me in amusement.

"What?" I asked.

"I cannot help but think of a quote from the Victorian author Elizabeth Gaskell. *There is always a pleasure in unraveling a mystery, in catching at the gossamer clue which will guide to certainty.*' You are a marvel to watch, Charli. You definitely have a magical knack for finding things, including clues," he complimented. "It's a wonder that you don't make a living at it, for if you did, you'd be the first I would hire."

Juniper arrived at the station and flung herself at Horatio. I left the two to their lives and headed back inside. To my surprise, Mason waited at the front desk for me.

"You had something you wanted to add?" he asked.

Too surprised to respond with words, I nodded.

The detective escorted me back to his office and closed the door. He offered the seat in front of his desk, but I refused, choosing to stand. I paced around while he sat down in his chair and leaned back, waiting.

"Horatio thinks that you are going with the simplest explanation, which is why you think he might have killed Mrs. K," I started.

"Occam's razor. I'm familiar with the philosophy. However, that doesn't always present the actual truth. I will follow the evidence where it leads, Charli." He paused to give me the floor again.

"But that's the thing. There is evidence that already proves he didn't do it."

"Like what?" challenged Mason.

"The blood on the fingertips and under the fingernails. Mrs. K scratched at whoever did this to her," I said with excitement.

Mason leaned forward on his desk. "I'll wait for the doc to make that discovery official. But what do you think it means?"

"It means that whoever did this should have scratches on their arms. And Horatio did not. On top of which, he's a troll." I noted my friend's biological status as a benefit. "His skin is so tough that it would take more than a fingernail to breach it."

The detective lifted an eyebrow in appreciation. "That's an astute observation. One that I had already made, however, which is why he is going home rather than spending the night here."

"Oh." I couldn't think of anything else to say in defense of my friend. I stopped pacing and sat down.

"Was there something else?" Mason pushed.

I opened my mouth a couple of times to try and breach the barrier between us. Unable to muster up enough courage, I closed my mouth.

Mason relaxed into the back of his chair with a sigh. He folded his hands in front of his face, his fingers tapping on his mouth. "Listen, I'm sorry for my demeanor back there in the library. It caught me off guard to find you with another dead body."

"I promise, I don't go looking for them," I said.

"I don't know. Two dead bodies in the time I've been here, and both times, you've somehow been involved."

"At least this time, I'm pretty sure I don't have a death curse trying to take my life," I joked.

"Probably not," admitted Mason. "But your involvement with the body could have been noticed by the person who committed the crime. Did you think of that?"

The detective had me on that point. "No."

"Well, I did. You shouldn't be involved. It could put you at risk. Any help you give me or the department could put you at risk." His voice softened. "That's the last thing I want to do."

"Is that why you stopped asking me to help? It's been ages since we..." I trailed off. The more he pushed me away, the more I was certain that I had imagined any connection to him in the first place.

"Partially that. And more my behavior at that one event," he added.

He caught my attention. "Which one?"

"The one with your cupid friend, Skeeter."

My eyes widened at his confession. "Are you talking about the one with the lemonade? Mason, nobody that was involved was in their right mind. I don't think anyone could be held responsible for their actions that night."

Affected by many love potions mixed together that had gone wrong, both Dash and Mason had clashed over my attention. Although I questioned the validity of their professed emotions at the time, I didn't take anything that was said that evening seriously. However, the detective's regret for his actions at the time surprised me.

"Whatever happened, Mason. It doesn't matter," I insisted.

"But it does, Charli. This job comes with its downfalls. If I want to do it right, then I need to make it my focus. I can't let any obstacles get in my way."

My heart sank like a rock. "And that's what I am to you? An obstacle?"

"No. Yes. I don't know what I mean." Mason wiped his face with his hands.

"Are you trying to say that Sheriff Big Willie can't do his job because he's married and has kids? Or what about my brother? He has a wife and a baby on the way," I pointed out.

"And that's great for them. But for me, it has never worked out." He frowned at his admission.

"Having a wife?" I pushed.

"Almost. I had a fiancée, and that ended, well..." He stopped talking.

The new information about the detective's past bowled me over. "What happened?" I asked in a small voice.

Mason stood up. "I think we're done here, Miss Goodwin."

"For good?" My eyes got a little glassy.

"For now."

Chapter Seven

When I hopped on my bike to head over to Nana's house, a little orange streak blurred its way in my direction. Peaches rubbed her furry face against my leg, her demanding little body insisting she come with me.

"You want to visit your old buddy?" I asked, picking her purring body up. In answer, she leaped into the basket on the front of the bike, her tiny body disappearing as she settled in until her head popped up.

Once I got us on the road, I pedaled my way to my grandmother's house without using the magic and enjoyed the exertion of energy. The faster my legs went, the more Peaches enjoyed the wind ruffling through her fur. As I approached the house, nostalgia squeezed my heart.

It had been a hard decision to move out of Nana's, my

home for so much of my life, including some of the most important events so far. I missed being woken up by her teasing in the morning, maybe more so than her incredible cooking. Returning now made me feel like an outsider. Like I had taken all of my secrets with me, and the only place I belonged was sitting in the formal parlor. Grabbing Peaches out of the bike basket, I trudged up the porch steps and knocked on the screen door.

"Get your behind in here, Birdy," Nana called out. "Stop acting like this isn't still your home."

With a creak and groan, the screen door pulled open, and I stepped inside, the comfort of the place wrapping itself around me like a warm blanket. The scent of something baking made my mouth water, and I followed its path to the kitchen. My cat pushed against me and rocketed out of my arms to greet Loki, my grandmother's gray-striped jerk of a cat. Maybe my kitty's presence would keep him from biting my ankles, and I enjoyed watching the two of them greet each other with sniffs and licks.

It took me a second to take in the scene around me. Cooking and baking implements scattered about every single surface. Flour, oil, and other ingredients dotted the landscape. Plates of various baked goods were stacked on every free surface. By the looks of the dirty pans on top of the stove, I'd bet that the fridge was full as well. Always a stickler for cleanliness, my grandmother's stress levels must be hitting a new high based on the entire scene.

"Nana, is everything okay?" I asked with caution.

My grandmother slammed the oven door. "Don't say anything. I know, I know, but it's the only thing that keeps me from blowing things up with my magic."

"That bad, hey?" It had been since my dad's death that she'd been this affected.

Nana placed her hands on her hips. "Child, I don't think anything has been as bad as it is right now since before you came to us. And back then, I was a much younger woman. Of course, I'm pretty sure I aged a few years in the past day or so." She wiped a bead of sweat from her brow.

Without hesitation, I rushed to her and wrapped my arms around her. Normally, she was the one who consoled me with her epic embraces. But if I could give her a fraction of the compassion she'd offered me throughout my life, then maybe I could make a dent in her anxiety. She melted into me and hugged back with fierce pressure. I'd risk losing consciousness from lack of oxygen any day to help this woman that I loved so dear.

"I'll be fine," she muffled into my shoulder.

I rubbed her back. "Is there anything I can do to help?"

She squeezed me hard, patted my behind, and pulled away so she could look me in the eye. "Eat as much as you can while you're here and take a lot home with you?" A wry chuckle followed her request, and she sniffed. "Frosted fairy wings, I'm a mess, aren't I?"

It ruffled me to see her in such disarray. The woman had been a solid rock for as long as I could remember. Even with the death of both of my parents, she had remained the solid foundation from which I built my structure of support. Yet, I saw her now as a flawed being like anyone else, and it was freaking me out. Drawing on all of my strength, I hid my panic.

"I think you have reasons to be a little worried. A lot's been going on."

"You're telling me." Nana lifted the bottom of her apron and wiped underneath her eyes, smearing a little flour across her cheek in the process. "Big Willie was here this morning, filling me in on Eugenia. I knew that woman was a few spells short of sanity, but I had no idea she was so far gone. That outburst on the stage took me by surprise."

"It took us all by surprise, Nana." Picking up a lemon bar, I bit into the tangy treat. "But seeing her there on the library floor like that doesn't make any sense either."

My grandmother narrowed her eyes at me. "The sheriff told me that you had been there. Being around dead bodies like that is getting to be a habit with you. One I wish you'd lose as quick as lightnin'."

"It wasn't by choice." I proceeded to tell her everything that had happened up until my confrontation with Mason in his office.

"I'll admit, you do have a way of finding things. Apparently, clues, too. So you think whoever did it wanted to make Horatio look guilty?" she asked.

"Why else would they bring the body there, and include the poem about change?" I'd recited what I could of the Longfellow lines, enough for her to get the idea.

"Maybe they were trying to make a statement about the elections," suggested my grandmother.

"That's one heck of a statement. And I haven't seen that kind of protest around here anyway." None of the pieces of the entire puzzle made sense to me yet.

Nana pulled out the chair from the table and collapsed into it. "That's because I'm mighty good at my job. Nothing has been out in the open, but the council has received numerous complaints over these past few months."

"From who?" I demanded.

She shook her head. "Not your business. And besides, sometimes the notes were anonymous. Everyone here has a right for their voice to be heard. We all knew that making any changes would come with resistance. It's why we tried things out like the farmers' market."

"And the new stop signs at that one intersection, which I think everyone appreciated after the almost-accident," I added.

"Yes, but everyone wanted that. It's too soon for an election and a new council seat, but with the addition of Nora..." My grandmother trailed off, staring out the window, her brow furrowed.

For the first time, my grandmother looked her true age, a little tired and more worn down. "You got pressure from Hollis and Nora, didn't you?"

My grandmother pursed her lips. "Can't tell you that. Not unless you want to throw your hat into the ring and try to win the election."

"Sounds like a dangerous proposition," I attempted to joke back with her. When she didn't crack a smile, I asked a more serious question. "Are you going to go through with the election now? You know, considering the dead body and all."

"That's what's got me cooking." She gestured around the kitchen. "I have to make the final decision today."

"And what's your first instinct?" My grandmother's gut never failed her in the past, but she had always had more support on the council when Uncle Tipper was still alive.

"There's what I want versus what my gut tells me. I want to delay the election until we find what happened with Eugenia. Or maybe until everyone is more prepared for bigger changes." She took a sticky cinnamon bun in her hand and unrolled it bit by bit. "But my gut tells me that stopping this election will do more harm than good at this point."

"But harm's already been done," I exclaimed. "Do you think Horatio can still run after all this? He may not be guilty, but in a small town like ours, sometimes rumors are stronger than the truth."

"And that will be his battle to fight, not yours, although I love how loyal you are to your friends. Let's talk about something else. Tell me why you came here in the first place." Nana licked her fingers clean of frosting.

My grandmother's ability to dig beneath the surface and find the truth in my life was uncanny. I never could hide anything from her, but maybe that was why I'd come to her today. As tired and distracted as she was, she didn't need to be burdened by my problems. "I wanted to see you."

"Birdy, look at me." She waited for me to comply. "There is absolutely nothing in this world that will get in my way of taking care of me and my own. You hear me?"

I nodded, a lump forming in my throat.

Nana got up from the table and opened the fridge. After she poured some iced tea into glasses, she ushered me into the living room, and we both sat down in our favorite places. "Now, tell me, is it seein' Eugenia that has you frazzled?"

Taking a sip, I pondered the question. "No, it wasn't pleasant, but it didn't really bother me."

"And that's a problem to discuss for another time. Then what's got your feathers all ruffled?" she asked.

I feared to tell her my concerns about not being able to find Raif's pug. Anytime something went wrong with my magic, Nana forced her own particular cure on me in the form of a disgusting, awful, horrible gray slime that she made me drink. Valuing my taste buds, I skipped over those fears. "Has Matt told you anything about Mason? Like is there something going on in his life to bother him?"

Nana failed to hide her grin. "So it's man troubles then?"

"No," I protested, heat flooding my cheeks. "It's just that when I spoke with him, he acted all strange and different."

"You mean, he's been avoiding you. I don't think you need your powers to find the reason why, Birdy. When did things change with him?" she asked.

I shrugged my shoulders. "I don't know."

"Yes, you do," Nana wheedled. "The man's embarrassed. I've heard more details of Skeeter's event than the ones I heard when I helped save the day. I'd bet the price of a phoenix feather that your detective acted less than noble when he was under the influence."

"But everyone was. It shouldn't change anything."

"But it did." Nana leaned forward in her favorite chair. "Think about it. Aren't Lee and Alison Kate together? And Ben and Lily?"

I dismissed her evidence with a shake of my head. "But they would have always gotten together at some point."

"What about Horatio and Juniper? That's about as unlikely a pairing as ever I would have figured, but here we are in a world where a giant troll has the hots for a tiny fairy."

"And both of them running in an election," I added.

"Right? So if you follow the clues, then you have to conclude that perhaps the detective revealed more of himself to you than he desired to at that moment. And if you'd open yourself up to *that* possibility, then maybe you can take some pity on the poor man and give him some distance to figure things out."

I squinted at my grandmother. "You just want me to stay away from the investigation of Mrs. K's murder."

Nana took a long sip of her iced tea in response.

"And he's not *my* detective. But he is keeping me out of the loop." I flashed back to our work together to solve Uncle Tipper's murder. We'd made a great team.

As if reading my mind, Nana spoke up. "But he had a reason to work with you, to save your life. This time, I'm grateful that you don't have to be involved." Sadness shadowed her eyes. My near-death experience had also taken a toll on my grandmother.

Thankfully, the timer on the stove dinged and interrupted our conversation. "That would be the brown sugar pound cake. Come on, let's check to see if it's done, and you can help me by making the caramel frosting to drizzle."

The rest of my troubles could wait. Besides, I could use the calorie-packed cake as fuel for what came next.

Chapter Eight

"I don't like this," complained Beau as we approached the retirement home together.

"What? The fact that I'm coming with you to your preferred dating spot or that you're helping me infiltrate the place so I can do some snooping?" I asked.

"Both. If they catch you, then they might ban me from ever coming back," the vampire whined.

"Are you more concerned about your dating status than finding out what happened to a woman who lost her life? Beau, I never took you for someone so heartless," I accused.

His pudgy face drooped in guilt. "You're right. Let's go."

I might have laid the guilt on a little bit too thick, but I needed an excuse to get inside. While the wardens focused on Mrs. K's body, I could go through her room and see if anything in there gave any indication of who might have wanted to hurt her. I stopped Beau just shy of the entrance and pulled him to the side of the building. "Maybe we shouldn't sign me in." Thoughts of leaving hard evidence of my presence worried me. "Can't you do something to sneak me inside?"

"Like what?" he asked.

"Don't vampires have the ability to make humans do what they want? Isn't that one of your superpowers?"

Beau crossed his arms. "I never took you for someone so simpleminded, Charli." He mimicked my tone from before, laying the guilt at my feet. "Of course all vampires have the same abilities you've seen on television or in movies, right?"

"No?" I replied with sheepish hesitation.

"Do you have the same magical talents as your brother or your grandmother?" he asked.

"No."

"It's the same for vampires. There are many of us who can live without taking much blood from others to survive. And only a small percentage of vampires can't exist in daylight." He admonished me with a disappointed expression on his face.

"I'm sorry, Beau." Remorse churned my stomach for pushing him and for my assumptions about his undead life.

"Thanks." He peeked through a side window. "Oh good, Alice is at the front desk. It shouldn't be hard to get you in. She has a thing for me, you know?"

"How is it that in some aspects of life, you are a bumbling fool and in others—"

"I'm a serious Don Juan Casanova? As I said, we all possess different talents." He smiled a fangy grin at me.

Beau sweet-talked his way in without signing the book, claiming he wanted to introduce me to Cordelia. After Alice flirted shamelessly with him, offering to finish anything Cordelia couldn't, I pasted a smile on to hide my abject disgust. We both climbed the stairs to the rooms on the second floor.

"Which one is Mrs. K's room?" I whispered to my roommate.

He pointed down the hall. "Last one on the left. When she had her panic attack, they said that the nurses found her out on the roof of the porch that wraps around underneath her window."

"So there would be an easy way to get in and out of her room without detection?" I asked.

Beau shrugged but didn't offer any other insights when he heard his name shrieked out in glee. Running his hand through the few strands of hair on his head, the vampire changed his attitude in an instant. "Cordelia," he purred. "My darling."

"Quick, let's get you inside my room before the other girls find out you're here." The thin older lady gazed at him in absolute adoration.

Beau gestured at me. "But I want to introduce my roommate to you, Miss Charli Goodwin."

Cordelia paid me no attention. "Yes, yes. Nice to meet you. Come on, Beau. We've got almost half an hour before the

women in the quilting bee will miss me and come lookin'."
She licked her lips in anticipation, and I turned on my heel,
sprinting for Mrs. K's room. I didn't need any more horrors to
be stuffed into my head to fuel more nightmares.

I half-expected a warden's protection to be blocking the
door. With the absence of any, I blessed my luck and tried the
doorknob. It turned freely, and I nudged the door open. Not
locked. Wanting to get inside to escape detection, I folded my
body through the small opening I'd created and slipped into
the darkened room.

It reeked of gardenias, and the sense memory of the scent
and the odor of her dead body came back, turning my
stomach again. After a few seconds to compose myself, I
opened my eyes and let them adjust to the light. All of her life
existed in this tiny space. A twin bed on the left was still
unmade, the quilted comforter pooled on the floor beside it.

In the far corner by the window sat a large desk.
Memories of the same piece of furniture sitting at the front of
a classroom came back to me. She had taken a token of her
teaching days with her, holding onto what was important to
the very end.

With my eyes adjusting, I noticed that all the decorations
in the room were from her classroom. A map of the United
States was tacked up over her desk. Motivational posters that
she used to quote to us hung on the walls, their tattered edges
rolling up a bit. As much as we made fun of her for her
passion for our town, the woman had brought the same level
of enthusiasm to all of her teachings.

A wave of sadness crashed over me at the thought of someone taking her life. I wondered how long they would leave her stuff there until they boxed it up and put it away as if she never existed. As far as I knew, she had no family, calling all of us kids *hers*. And we all grew up and left. But a part of her never did.

Shaking off the grief that she was due, I conjured a ball of light. I searched all the nooks and crannies for anything out of the ordinary. Crawling on the floor, I saw nothing underneath her bed.

I wrinkled my nose when I got to her laundry hamper. The stench of her cloying perfume choked me. I started to back away but caught a glint of something in the basket. Digging through the clothes and attempting to ignore the possibility that I might be touching her dirty undies, I felt around for what I thought I'd seen.

"Eureka," I whispered, grasping a glass bottle.

My hand would stink of the spilled perfume for weeks, I thought. How did this get in here?

Standing up, I searched for a nearby place where it might have been. On the top of her antique wooden dresser, a dark-ringed stain stood out on its surface. Leaning down and taking a whiff, I confirmed that the perfume bottle had been here before it was spilled and fell into the laundry basket. Not much else sat on top of the surface, which was unusual for an impeccable Southern woman, but maybe what she cherished most rested on her old desk.

I ran my hand over the wood and stepped closer to inspect

the dresser. My foot crunched on something. Peering down, I examined whatever was broken underneath. Reflections of my light bounced off the remains of the glass of a mirror. A silver handle poked out from underneath the dresser. A matching brush lay nearby, almost as if both pieces had been on top of the dresser and knocked off.

I guessed that there'd been a struggle here, making the room the potential scene of her actual death. At least maybe my efforts would put Horatio in the free and clear. No way could a troll have made it into the room without being heard or seen. And his massive presence wouldn't have fit very well. But whoever had attacked Mrs. K, surely they'd committed the murder here and deliberately moved her. But why?

The door slammed open, and I jumped, dropping the perfume bottle from my hand. "Charli. I should've known." Mason glared at me in disapproval.

"I'm here visiting a friend?" I attempted.

"Don't tell me. You excused yourself to go to the bathroom and somehow found yourself in a murder victim's room instead? How lucky for you." He crossed his arms.

"What are you doing here?" I asked.

"Do you think so little of my skills that I wouldn't have already searched this room? I purposefully didn't cast a warden's protection on it because it occurred to me that perhaps the killer might return to the scene of the crime. And here you are."

"You know I didn't do it," I scoffed.

Mason stared me down until something caught his

attention. He sniffed and stepped closer to me. "Why do you smell like that?"

I pointed at the bottle on the floor. "Her perfume."

"Did you pick that up yourself? Charli," he admonished.

Pixie poop. "I found it in her clothes hamper. There's a stain on top of the dresser where it probably sat before it was knocked off."

"I know," said Mason.

"And a hand mirror and brush look like they flew off the dresser in a struggle, too," I added.

"Again, I know, Charli."

"How do you know?" I challenged.

"Because I've already done a thorough sweep of the room, taking notes from everything." He produced his pad.

"Then why wasn't it cordoned off?"

Mason's eyes burrowed into me. "Because I set up an alarm spell to alert me if anyone came in. I thought that maybe the culprit might return to the scene to clean up his or her tracks. I get here and find you right in the middle of things. Even when I instructed you to stay out of it."

He had me. There was no excuse I could produce that would get me out of trouble. I raised my hands and shrugged my shoulders. "Curiosity?"

"It killed the cat and could get you into trouble," he countered.

"I'm used to that," I said.

"I wish you weren't." The detective sighed. "Fine. Did you find anything else worthy of note?"

I shook my head. "I was kind of hoping I would pinpoint something that didn't belong. That way I could test it and see if it led me somewhere."

"You are hoping to find an item off the murderer that would take you straight to him or her?" Mason blew out a hard breath. "You really have no sense of safety, do you?"

"I hadn't gotten that far in my plans," I admitted. "Plus, you know my limitations. Finding a person is a lot harder for me than finding an object."

"So, what you're saying is that your skills may not be helpful at the moment and that maybe you should leave the job to someone say, oh, more like me?" He pointed at himself.

"Fine," I huffed. "You win." I held up my hand like a common criminal in surrender.

"I sincerely doubt that you're giving me anything other than a victory in this small moment." He escorted me to the door. "I'm going to have to reseal the room again."

"I'm sorry I gave you more work to do," I teased. Before I left, I took his hand in mine. "Promise me you will call me if there is anything I can find for you."

He pulled away from my touch. "The only thing I want you to search for is your way home and the ability to stay out of my investigation." He wrinkled his nose. "And maybe some soap and water to wash off that scent."

I sniffed my hand and cringed. "I don't think I'll ever be able to have gardenias in my house." I made my way down the hall, bypassing Cordelia's room and ignoring the grunts and giggles coming from behind the closed door.

Chapter Nine

Whenever I attempted to use my magic to find any evidence of Uncle Tipper's participation in my adoption, I only drained myself of spent energy. Perhaps the papers I longed for didn't exist, or maybe, like finding a needle in a haystack, I might have to clear out the house of more junk before my magic would work.

I toiled through an entire day, sifting through piles and piles of stuff with no more success than a few full trash bags. At least the task at hand kept me busy and stopped me from obsessing about Mrs. K. By now, the entire town was focused more on who had killed the old teacher than on the election. Based on the rumors floating about, Horatio's chances in the election were slim to none, and none just rode out of town on the back of a unicorn.

"I think you need some help," suggested Beau, interrupting my thoughts.

I rubbed the back of my neck. "It's getting to be a bigger task than I thought it would be. Even with your help, it could take years to go through everything."

My roommate opened up one of the trash bags to sift through what I was tossing. "What about your friend's service? Or maybe Juniper's too busy with the election and her boyfriend currently in hot water."

I shrugged. "She does have a crew that works for her, although I'm not sure I would trust anybody but her to go through the paperwork. You do have a point, though. I can't go through the entire house alone. I'll check with her. It might be worth the money to at least organize the chaos."

Beau eyed the small space clean from the debris that surrounded me in the room. "I agree. Oh, and you have a piece of mail waiting for you downstairs."

When I got to the first floor, I found the thick cream envelope sitting on top of a side table with my name written in fancy calligraphy. I dreaded opening it, but throwing it away wouldn't change what waited inside. With a sigh, I ripped the expensive paper open and pulled out the invitation announcing the engagement party for Tucker Hawthorne and my cousin Clementine.

No one knew about the conversation between Tucker and me when he confessed he still had feelings for me before I took off to find his business partner and guilty murderer Ashton at Tipper's house. I'd closed the door on the chapter of my life that included him, and he chose to walk through the rest of his with my cousin. I hoped that he found happiness in his choice, but I would never be able to conjure up anything more than good wishes.

Giving in to a darker mood, I trudged into the kitchen and poured myself a tall glass of iced tea. Carrying it out to the porch, I plopped down into one of the rockers, staring out into the glow of the day's sunset. A black dot in the sky winged its way in my direction, and the caws that called out as it got closer stopped the flood of my heavy thoughts. Tipper's crow, Biddy, circled and descended until she landed on the porch railing, flapping her wings and squawking at me.

"Hey there, Miss Biddy," I cooed at her. "How you doin'?"

The bird cocked her head to the side to regard me with her bright yellow eye. She cawed in odd syllables, holding up her end of the conversation.

"Oh, me? I guess I've been better," I admitted to the crow. I don't suppose you know where Tipper kept all his secrets hidden?"

The bird hopped on the railing but gave away no hints. With a light flap of her wings, Biddy fluttered to the rocking chair beside me, Tipper's usual place to enjoy some sweet tea.

"I miss him, too." Even if he wasn't all there in his head, the old man had given pretty decent advice, and I could use any help I could get right now. As if sensing my sadness, the crow hopped over and lit on my shoulder much like she used to with my great-uncle. Her head nudged under my chin. And I scratched her dark feathers with the tip of my finger.

"Thanks, girl." The two of us rocked on the porch together until the last orange rays of the sun decorated the sky.

⚜

WHEN I OPENED the door that evening to answer an incessant knocking, a strong hand grabbed my arm and pulled me outside. I shrieked and fought against the perpetrator, beating my fists into strong muscles.

Dash snickered at my efforts. "Feeling feisty tonight, are we?"

Adrenaline pumped through my veins, and I smacked his arm. "Far from it."

He picked up my hand and sniffed it. "Why do you smell like that awful odor from the other night?" I'd done my best to scrub off the remains of Mrs. K's fragrance from my hand, but his sensitive nose still picked up on the few particles left behind.

"I spilled some perfume before, and guess I didn't get it all off. What are you doing here?" My diversion question came out sharper than I had intended.

"I think someone needs to have some fun, and I've heard there's a place nearby where you can let loose a little." He pointed out into the darkness of the yard.

"Where?" I didn't have the energy to pull myself together and make an effort.

Dash touched the frown lines on my forehead and

attempted to smoothe them out. "Stop your fussin'. I promise you'll have fun. And it's within walking distance."

I appreciated the wolf shifter's efforts to cheer me up, but the heavy tiredness of depression still clung to me. "Not tonight," I refused. "But thanks anyway."

"If you don't come with me now, there will be a group of invaders that will descend upon your house and drag you out. Which is scarier?" To make me laugh, he pulled his animal to the surface, his eyes glowing amber, and fangs growing in his toothy grin, sharp and long. "Of course, I could always kidnap you myself," he rasped, his voice teetering between man and beast.

I conjured up a tiny ball of crackling energy in my hand and tossed it at him in play. It whizzed right by his head, almost scorching off some of his beard. The magic sizzled and went out in the darkness of night. "Careful. I can be scary, too."

"I like a challenge." Dash wiggled his eyebrows, a smug smile still spread on his lips.

I found myself chuckling despite my bad mood. "You're not going to leave me alone, are you?"

He shook his head. "Surrender or be taken. Those are your options."

While I contemplated my options, Dash scooped me up and threw me over his shoulder. "Took too long," he declared.

I thrashed about in his grasp, and he swatted my behind. "Behave, or you might get yourself hurt."

Conjuring up an easy hex I used to use on Matt, I aimed my magic at the wolf shifter's firm backside and let loose.

"Ow," he cried out, setting me down on the ground and rubbing the offended area. "That hurt."

"Told you. I can be fierce when I want to be."

"Duly noted."

No longer being carried by a shifter with better night vision than me, I couldn't tell which way to go. Dash took my hand in his and led the way. A whinnying sound and the bucking against a wooden door alerted me to our proximity to the barn.

"They're noisy tonight," I exclaimed.

"They can sense me," said Dash. "Horses and wolves don't necessarily make the best friends. They're smart enough to sense the danger, unlike some girls who seem not to get enough." He squeezed my hand.

I gulped, and let the implication of his words float into the night air, joining the chirping of the cicadas.

As we reached the edge of the property, light from inside the shed ahead lit a small area around it. Laughter and voices from inside beckoned us. When we got closer, I pulled my hand away from Dash's, unwilling to deal with any questions or teasing. I immediately missed his warm touch.

"Finally," Blythe huffed in a dramatic fashion. "We were getting ready to storm the castle."

An orange object blurred past me and pounced into the middle of the room. Peaches had followed us from the house, thrilled to have playmates in the old shed. She rubbed herself on everyone's legs and got down to the serious business of chasing shadows and dust mice.

"Now that we're all here, I can pass out the party favors." Lee placed a small device in each of our hands except Dash's.

"You don't get one?" I asked him.

He dug something out of his pocket and pulled out a similar looking rectangle. "I already have one."

"Is this what Mrs. K was talking about in her crazy rant?" asked Lily.

"Yes," replied Lee. "Although I got on Daddy's back for talkin' about it out in public, especially since I haven't perfected it yet."

"I know what they are," I said. "They're called mobile phones."

In my experience in the world outside of Honeysuckle, most of the magical community stayed away from human technology. Although there were spells to protect any devices from frying when used, magic and the more intricate electronics of today's devices didn't mix well. Unless they lived in a large city with a massive contingency of humans and magical beings living in tandem, most magic wielders avoided human technology. It surprised me that Lee wanted to mess with it.

"Dash and I found a huge stash of these on one of our last runs," Lee explained.

The two friends liked to go scrapping for parts all over. According to the shifter, he was still searching for a replacement part for my dad's old motorcycle.

With breathy excitement, Lee displayed his treasure. "These phones seem to be out of date with current human technology, but I think they'll work just fine for us." The tech genius flipped the top piece of plastic to reveal a keypad underneath.

Dash took a similar gadget out of his pocket. "To be honest, they're a bit on the ancient side. I miss the one I got rid of when I moved here because the dang thing wouldn't work. Shifters don't have problems with human tech like you witches do." After an alarming noise rang out, he flipped the device open, pressed the button in the center, and held it up to his ear. "Hey, Lee."

Ben glanced between the two guys. "So it's a communication device? But how are you powering it without blowing its circuits with your magic?"

"Are those already spelled?" I asked, remembering the phones the last tracker I worked with had used.

Lee pushed his glasses up his nose. "I think I figured out a different way to make them operate in Honeysuckle. They tap into the same magic that protects our town. For now, they won't function outside of here, but within our borders, they'll give us a way to communicate with each other faster. If you scroll through the menu, you'll see that I've already programmed all of your numbers so that all you have to do is scroll and select who you want to call." He launched into a more detailed explanation, and we followed along, trying to keep up.

"So instead of cell phones, you've created *spell* phones," I announced. "Leland Chalmers, Jr., has anyone told you lately that you're brilliant?"

Alison Kate grabbed him by his cheeks and planted a quick kiss on his lips. "I have," she gushed.

We spent the next half-hour calling each other back and forth until we understood how to use the devices.

"Right now, the only ones that work are here in this room," Lee declared. "But if y'all can help me test things out and make improvements, I may be able to make them work for our entire community." Our friend accepted all of the heaps of praises and congratulations for his idea in embarrassed humility.

"I think it's awesome, Lee, but I have one more question. How come Alison Kate has a sparkly purple one while the rest of us have these drab gray or black ones?" I teased.

Lavender agreed, pouting and plotting how to decorate hers with flowers.

Dash leaned his muscled body into me. "I'll scrounge whatever color you want."

His intense sincerity shut down any playful question of doubt that rested on the tip of my tongue. I swallowed hard and nodded.

"I can't believe Mrs. K would disapprove of an idea like this," exclaimed Ben, holding up his phone.

"I know, but that's only part of what makes her death weird. I want to get Charli's opinion," Lily added. "What do you think about Mrs. Kettlefields?"

Clearly, I had arrived in the middle of an ongoing

discussion. Whatever I said next, I needed to avoid letting them know about my excursion to her room at the retirement home.

"Don't you think it's strange that she would be against the election?" asked Lavender. "I wasn't close enough to read her aura, but something seemed off."

"Has your grandmother told you anything?" Alison Kate pressed.

I attempted to placate some of their questions and hold them off. "Nana has a lot on her plate right now. Between the dead body on the one hand and those who want the election on the other, she's caught in the middle, trying to figure out what to do." None of my friends needed to know that the leader of our town was struggling to keep things together. "But I'm sure if she thinks the election should continue, then everything will work out as it should."

"Said like a true politician. All words and no answers," Ben teased. "But what do you really think?"

Blythe narrowed her eyes at me. "She knows something. I just know it," she accused.

"Fine," I breathed out. "But this goes no further than these four walls. Witch's honor, y'all." I pointed around the room at each one of them.

"What about me?" Dash challenged. "I'm no witch."

"True, but you're a man of honor," I said.

He scoffed. "Or so I have you fooled."

I pointed a finger in the shifter's face. "Then swear to me

in any manner you want that you won't share what I'm about to tell you."

The corners of Dash's lips curled in amusement. "You mean something like, cross my heart and hope to die. Stick a needle in my eye?" He traced an *X* over his heart as he said the words.

The rest of my friends laughed at his attempt.

"Try this." I conjured another crackling ball of energy in my hand. "Repeat after me. *I swear on this ball so shiny, if I tell what's said here, you'll hex my hiney.*"

"Seriously?" growled Dash.

"Or I could zap you right here, right now," I offered.

He gave in, and repeated the words, adding a cross of his heart for good measure.

I filled everyone in on my infiltration of Mrs. K's room. They agreed with me it was more likely she had been attacked there rather than at the library.

"Do you think the wardens are close to figuring out who did it?" Ben asked.

I shook my head. "I don't think so. Right now, their biggest suspect is also the least likely."

"That hasn't stopped my little sister from implicating Horatio." Lily frowned at the mention of Linsey.

"And the detective's not asking for your help?" Blythe pushed.

Dash scowled at the floor. "Perhaps he thinks she should stay away from a possible murder."

"But I can help," I whined in protest.

Continuing, we went through the possibilities of who might have wanted to hurt our old teacher. Even though each of us had stories about her, we couldn't think of a reason why a former student would have waited to take their revenge now.

"What about one of the other candidates? I'd bet all the money I don't actually have, placing the body in the library was meant to throw suspicion on Horatio," Lily surmised.

"And Juniper's his girlfriend. I can't imagine her being capable of even hurting a flea," I said. "Flint is too sensible. Now, Raif?"

Everyone agreed that my least favorite vampire was the one in most opposition to Mrs. K's points.

I blew out a breath. "The problem with her death is that it's weird."

Ben scoffed. "I don't think I've ever heard a murder described that way in all my time as an advocate. But Charli's right. None of it makes sense, and the fact that there isn't a clear suspect is troublesome."

Dash jumped into the conversation. "It means that anyone involved in the investigation could put themselves at risk."

I turned to take him head-on. "And maybe the risk is worth taking if it means keeping friends from being hurt."

"At what expense, Charli?" The wolf shifter raised his voice. "You just got your life back not too long ago. Now you're willing to put it on the line again?"

"If that's what it takes to keep the wrong person from being accused, then yes," I countered.

Dash cocked an eyebrow at me. "I thought you said the troll was taken out of consideration. If that's true, then there's nothing for you to do but stay out of things."

"For the time being, he's not arrested. But if I can help find the actual culprit, then everything can get back to normal. Isn't that worth a little risk?" I glanced around for support from my friends, and they all seemed busy with their new phones.

"Not if it means your life," shouted Dash. His irritation grew with the volume of his voice.

The air in the room sizzled with the shifter's magic, and the rest of my friends scrambled to their feet. Peaches scurried to plant herself in front of the shifter and hissed at him, her back bowed and her tail all fluffed out in irritation.

"Party's over," declared Lee, pushing his shifter friend out the door first.

After quick hugs outside, everyone left except Alison Kate who waited for Lee to finish calming Dash down.

"I'm fine," the wolf shifter bellowed.

Lee tapped his chest with his finger. "Make sure you stay that way. Charli, you want us to walk you back?" he offered.

Dash's amber eyes flashed in the dark. "I'll do it."

Lee waited for my response. "Charli?"

Not one particle of me wanted to hear any more lectures from a man telling me what I should or should not do. First, Mason cut me off with accusations that working together would be dangerous to me as well as to our whatever-we-were relationship. And now, Dash and his overprotective instincts threatened to tick me off.

Picking up my cat, I pulled her in tight to my chest. "I can make it on my own," I announced into the night air, and stomped off, bumping the shifter's arm with my own on purpose.

Dash followed a few steps behind me all the way back to my house in silence. By the time I climbed the porch steps and let Peaches out of my arms, I was ready for the night to be over.

"Charli, hold on a minute," he called out, stopping me from going inside.

I walked to the edge of the top step. "What?" I asked in exasperation.

"I didn't mean to tell you what to do. But I don't like it when you seem to run toward danger instead of fleeing from it."

"Not always," I protested.

"But if your instincts were wired the right way, then you would know better than to hang out with someone like me." Despite his words trying to push me away, he took a step closer.

A ball of nerves bounced around in my stomach at the spoken truth. "I like being with you."

"My point exactly." Dash closed the distance between us. "And if I were a stronger man, I would be able to stay away. But I like being around you, too." He closed the distance between us and pulled me down a step until his face was level with mine.

I didn't need any moonlight to sense his intense gaze. He lifted his hand and brushed my hair behind my ear, his finger stroking my cheek. "You're a trouble magnet, Charli Goodwin."

"I am who I am." I tried to convey so much in those simple words, but feared I failed.

He cupped my cheek. "I wouldn't have it any other way," he breathed.

My nerves tingled down to my toes in expectation. He leaned in, his hot breath blowing against my lips. I closed my eyes in sweet anticipation.

A fire alarm screeched into the air, and I squealed. My new spell phone lit up. Dash closed his eyes and backed away, giving me space.

Reading the name on the screen, I cursed Blythe under my breath. The heated moment fizzled and faded as I flipped the phone open and hit the button with a groan.

"I truly hate you."

Chapter Ten

Sitting on the stiff parlor sofa, I waited for Juniper to show me how much she would charge to help with the house. Numbers and figures sparkled in the air as she twirled her finger, figuring out the math.

"It's a big job, Charli. It might take my whole crew if you want it done fast. Or I can assign one or two of my girls to it, but it will take much longer. However, either way you want to do it, I think this is my assessment." She produced her wand and waved it, and a scroll rolled out of midair and floated into my hands.

"That's more than fair," I agreed.

With confidence, the fairy gave me her breakdown. "Based on what you told me, you want us to collect any obvious paperwork and organize it to give you an opportunity to go through it. All objects will be sorted by size and functionality, including grouping them down into piles of broken or not."

"About going through the paperwork, will you be one of the ones sorting?" I asked.

She quivered her wings and shook her head. "My schedule is just so full right now with the election and the other jobs I've scheduled. Why?"

I explained the nature of what I was looking for and requested her utmost secrecy.

"For a job like that, I highly recommend Moss. She used to work in an office building in another city, and might know what she's looking at in a glance," said Juniper.

"But do you trust her?" I didn't know the fairy well, and giving her full access to my house went against my gut.

"She's been working with me for over a year, and I have nothing but compliments about her thoroughness. If you want, I can provide recommendations." Juniper hovered in slight impatience. "I wish I could promise that I could do the job myself, but I'm doing my best not to spread myself too thin."

After a pause, I signed off on the estimate, and the scroll rolled up again, tying a binding red ribbon around itself. It would be a relief to have a more organized way to sift through the last of Tipper's life and begin to make the house my own. I trusted Juniper and her judgment. Plus, she promised she would be around to check in on her employees from time to time.

"How's Horatio doing?" I'd waited to ask the question I really wanted to.

Her wings trembled in agitation. "Not well. He attempts to keep his troubles away from me, but I know how hard he's struggling. It's taken him centuries to build his life away from his family and his kind. He's not welcome with them, and now he questions how long he'll be able to stay here in Honeysuckle after all of this."

"Will he be dropping out of the election?" I asked.

Juniper sniffed and wiped a tear away. "He doesn't think he has a choice. He may not be under arrest, but the damage has been done. I want to quit, too."

I gasped. "You can't give up yet."

"That's what Horatio says to me every day." She composed herself. "I'll stay in the race for as long as I can. I know it's important that everyone has a choice, although I think my chances may be tied to my sweetie more than he thinks."

"If there's anything I can do to help," I offered, standing up from the sofa.

"I know it's customary to start a job on a handshake, but..." The fairy fluttered over and kissed me on the cheek. "Thank you for your friendship."

I smiled at her. "Thank you for staying strong." I lifted my arm and bent it like she had the night of the speeches.

She scoffed. "I'm not really."

"I know a troll who would disagree."

WITH THE WORRIES about the state of my house gone, I rode my bike into town to have lunch at the cafe. Life's interruption the night before resulted in my agreement to check out the new drool-worthy man in town who supposedly came in every day and sat at the counter. I almost refused to go due to Blythe's timely interruption, but I owed her more loyalty than spite.

Before I walked into the Harvest Moon, I spotted Dash leaning on the side of the building. "You're late," he accused.

I stopped beside him. "How did you know I was coming here?"

He tapped his ear. "I'm a shifter. I keep telling you this, but you don't listen. I could hear the entire conversation."

"Because you were eavesdropping?"

"No, because of how close in proximity I was to you." He cocked an eyebrow at me, and my cheeks heated.

"Blythe isn't going to be happy that you're crashing our covert mission," I said.

"I know. That's why I have a built-in cover. Hey, man," Dash called out.

Lee approached and put his arm around both of us. "All good with the two of you?" he asked.

"Never better," replied Dash. He flashed me a teasing grin over Lee's head.

I placed a hand on my hip. "And how is bringing in another person going to serve as a cover?"

Dash mimicked my stance. "Relax. The two of us will take a table and let you sit at the counter. I'm just interested in checking out the competition for the current hot guy in town."

"Yeah, me too," joked Lee. He opened the door and walked inside.

Blythe's face brightened as she checked to see who came in. When she spotted the three of us, she furrowed her brow. Lee and Dash did as they promised and occupied a nearby table. I sat my behind down on a stool at the counter.

"What are they doing here?" she hissed.

"Note to self," I said. "Shifters have better senses of smell, hearing, and sight."

Blythe gazed at me in confusion. "What does that mean?"

"It means I won't be talking on my spell phone anywhere near him next time." The sound of a chuckle earned the wolf shifter a dirty look from me.

The bells on the door jingled, and Blythe's head whipped up again. The color in her cheeks deepened, and the eager smile that spread on her lips surprised me. "Hey, you," she practically purred. "I'd like to introduce you to one of my closest friends, Charli."

I swiveled the stool to get my first look at the specimen and gasped. "It's you."

Damien widened his eyes and took the seat next to me. "It seems we were destined to meet, you and I. Pardon me for my confusion, but I believe your name to be Charlotte, is it not?" he asked in his posh British accent.

Blythe jumped to answer for me. "Her name is actually Charlotte, but her friends call her Charli," she clarified.

"And which am I?" Damien asked with interest.

"I'm not sure yet." The same nagging recognition knocked at the back of my mind, but I still couldn't pinpoint why.

Perhaps his devilishly handsome looks made me nervous. I couldn't tell his true age from his facial features. Not one wrinkle marred his perfect skin. The symmetry of his face was pleasing, and he had a dimple in the middle of his chin that begged to be touched.

His plump lips broke into a smile, showing off his pointed fangs. "Then let me err on the side of hope and say that I am pleased to meet you, Charli." He took my hand in his and brought it to his mouth, planting a light kiss on my skin.

Simultaneously, my friend frowned behind the counter, and an audible growl rumbled from the nearby table. If only the animal in the man could sense my absolute lack of interest in the perfect specimen in front of me, he might not need to make his displeasure known with such volume. I pulled my hand away and folded it in my lap.

"Blythe, there are other customers in here," warned Mr. Steve from the pass-through window.

She gritted her teeth. "I'm on it," she called out. "I'll be right back," she promised Damien in a singsong tone too cheery to belong to her.

"Talk me up," she mouthed at me, taking out her pad to take orders.

The newcomer turned in his stool, so his entire body faced me. "I confess, I have been wanting to talk to you. Raif is absolutely useless when it comes to providing good intelligence on the citizenry of this quaint town."

Something about the way he described Honeysuckle rubbed me the wrong way. "I spent an entire year away from home, and I chose to return, especially for the town's charms."

He frowned. "Oh, dear, I fear I may have, how might you put it, stepped my foot into it. I, of course, am enjoying my time in Honeysuckle Hollow. I have traveled all over the world, and getting to know more about the small communities is what gives me the most pleasure. Especially when I find such interesting inhabitants in residence."

"Like Blythe?" I pushed.

"She has one of the most important jobs in town," he insisted.

"Really?"

"Yes. By serving each person who comes into the only food establishment, she exposes herself to everyone, and in turn is a wealth of knowledge. You could say that she is one of the most integral parts of your community." He accepted the glass of iced tea from Blythe with a nod and thanks, causing her to giggle as she offered refills to the other customers.

That nagging feeling in the back of my head wouldn't leave me alone, but I liked how he saw my friend as more than a waitress. She deserved someone who saw the best parts of her as I did.

"That's a nice way of describing her." Although he could

technically say the same thing about Sassy, I was glad that it wasn't the annoying fairy's shift right now.

Damien redirected our conversation. "I hope you have received an apology from my friend for his appalling behavior the other night with the temporary loss of his pet. I've never seen him act quite like that."

"I'm used to people questioning my talents. Especially when I'm the only one with them in town." I shrugged, stirring the ice in my tea with a straw.

"They are rare and wonderful. As I said, I have traveled the world, and if you possess the magic I think you do, then you could be making more than just a living elsewhere." He leaned in closer and lowered his voice with a cold glint in his eyes. "I know people who would pay good money."

Blythe rejoined us. "My ears are burning. You wouldn't happen to be telling him any stories about me would you, Charli?"

Damien straightened in his seat and turned to face my friend, his tone changing in a split second. "Only good things." He reached his hand out and covered hers resting on the counter.

It unnerved me to watch my friend's normally cool and guarded demeanor melt like ice on a hot summer's day. Her tittering giggles did me in. "I'm going to go join Dash and Lee, and give you two some space."

"But you haven't had lunch yet." Blythe pleaded with me with wide eyes to stay.

"Fine." I placed my elbows on the counter and held my head in my hands, enduring every flirtatious banter.

My friend never did take my order for food, and my stomach growled its displeasure. A plate of fries appeared in front of me.

Dash sat down on the accompanying empty stool and grabbed one, swiping it through the ketchup and cramming it in his mouth. "Here. I know you're hungry."

The way he sat so close to me made Damien take notice. He extended a hand. "I don't believe we've met. Damien Mallory."

"I heard. Dash Channing." He gripped hands with the vampire, holding onto him far too long with a challenging gaze.

"Down, boy," I admonished the shifter, who took an extra second to let go of the vampire.

Damien kept up a pleasant front but paid more attention to Blythe until he had to leave. He repeated reassurances that they would spend more time together soon.

Turning to Dash and me, he asked, "Would the two of you like to join my lady friend and I sometime in the near future?"

"The two of who?" I uttered, not wanting to really spend any time with the guy who creeped me out.

"You and your boyfriend," Damien clarified, indicating Dash.

I choked on a sip of tea. "I don't have a boyfriend."

Dash patted me on the back. "Hey, I'm a boy and a friend."

"Shut up," I hissed at him.

Blythe interrupted us. "Charli, you wouldn't mind going with us on a picnic, would you?"

"We'd love to," accepted Dash before I could decline.

I swiveled around to stare at the shifter. "What are you doing?"

"Making plans with your friend. Being social and taking an interest in the people of my town." He ate another fry, holding it in his teeth to show off his smug smile.

Relief swept through me when Damien stood up to leave.

The vampire took my hand in his and kissed it again. "It was nice getting to know a little more about you, Charli. I look forward to our double date." He gestured at the door. "Blythe, my dear, would you mind speaking with me outside?"

My friend weaved her way around the counter, ignoring all of the other hungry customers. I watched her through the glass door as she giggled and touched him. He kissed the back of her hand as well, but instead of yanking it away like I had, she pressed the skin to her lips. She floated back inside in a daze.

When she returned to the counter, I snapped my fingers in front of her face. "Who are you and what have you done with my friend?"

She tittered and clapped her hands. "I know, right? He's s-o-o-o cute. Whenever he's around, I can't seem to concentrate on anything else," she gushed.

"Frosted fairy wings, B, what happened to the girl who

said she would never be turned into a fool?" Hungry and annoyed, my last nerve threatened to walk out the door.

Blythe cupped my chin and looked at me with pity. "Maybe it took finding the right person to change my mind. If you had the courage to make a choice, you might find happiness, too." She let me go and went to pick up some lucky customer's order.

Out of spite, I pulled the plate of fries in front of me and ate the rest of them without letting the shifter have another one. Blythe returned with a full plate of food for me, but I still wasn't sure I could forgive her.

"When can we schedule our double date?" she asked.

"It's not a date," I complained.

"I'm counting it as one." Dash swiped a fresh fry from my plate.

I pointed a finger in his face. "You're already in enough trouble as it is, mister."

He ignored me and spoke to my friend. "I can take care of the main dish if one of you can do sides and the other brings dessert."

"I'll get Steve to let me bring the sides from here," volunteered Blythe.

"That leaves the dessert to you, Charli. I'll see you later." The shifter waved at both of us. "Can't wait for our date," he called out as he left.

"It's not a date," I yelled, causing the rest of the patrons in the cafe to stop talking and eating to stare at me.

"Yes, it is," Dash announced through the glass door with a wave and a wink.

I groaned loud and long. "You people are infuriating."

Blythe patted my head. "But you love us just the same." She walked away, humming out of key.

I didn't know who the *us* included, but at the moment, it did not consist of a certain stubborn furry-behinded shifter.

Chapter Eleven

Lee talked my ears off for the next half hour at the cafe, barely giving me a chance to finish my long-awaited lunch. He asked me every question under the sun about my experience with cell phones while I was away from Honeysuckle.

"Now, explain to me how they used to message each other with this," he said, holding up his flip phone.

"See the letters underneath the numbers?" I pointed. "If you hit those buttons enough times, the letters will show up on the screen, and you can spell out words. Using that method, you could create a message to send without calling."

"Fascinating, but what a waste of time. I think I can do something with that. What else?" he pushed.

Not having had a phone myself, my knowledge was limited. But I remembered one handy function when the tracker I was working with found a young boy hurt but still alive. "There's an emergency function on the phones that would put the person in touch with services that could come help." I winced at my poor explanation. "A quick way to dial directly in."

"An emergency button. Cool," he exclaimed. "I'll have to play with that. I wonder if I could hook the system up to the warden station? Or maybe find a way to turn the phone into a beacon of some sort."

"Like a homing signal?" I asked.

He nodded. "Something that would make it easy to locate whoever was in distress. Maybe that could save lives."

"It's a worthy project at least," I agreed. I didn't complain when Lee took off like a rocket to start tinkering and working through the many plans already formulated in his brain.

After finishing lunch and giving Blythe more grief about the upcoming picnic thing, I left the Harvest Moon and emerged into the afternoon sun, full and satisfied.

Ben stopped me on my way to my bike. "Charli, I'm glad I caught you. Would you mind stopping by the office for a moment?"

I followed my friend to the advocates' office, greeting Jed Farnsworth at his desk. Ben brought me to a lady sitting in a chair in front of the second desk.

"Hey, Ms. Alma. How are you doing?" I gave her a warm hug.

"I could be better, if I'm being honest." She patted my arm. "Did young Bennett fill you in on my dilemma?"

Ben took a seat behind his desk. "I did not, Ms. Lewis."

The older lady's face crumpled. "I'm afraid that I am missing some items of great worth from my possession. There's one item in particular that leaves me in great distress. I was wondering if I could hire you to help me find it." She opened the purse on her lap and dug through it, pulling out her wallet.

"You don't have to pay me, Ms. Alma. I'd be happy to help," I replied in confusion.

"Oh, but I overheard you talking with that good looking gentleman at the cafe that you could make money. I don't want you to think I don't value your talents. I can at least pay you a fee if you can locate the item," she offered.

I didn't want to argue in Ben and Jed's place of business. "When would you like me to try?"

Ben stood from his seat and circled around his desk. "I thought that maybe I would accompany you back to Ms. Lewis's house. As the missing items are a part of her will, I would like to be present, if you don't mind."

"Of course not," I assured my friend. Jed wished us luck, and the three of us headed out together.

When we got to her house, Ms. Alma relaxed a bit. "I didn't want to give any details while out and about. The one piece I am mainly concerned with is an emerald ring that my dear late husband gave me on the night of our honeymoon. It's a family heirloom on his side, and there has been more than a little drama about me having it. I intended to bequeath it to one of his sisters' children, but when I looked for it, I couldn't find it."

An easy task, I looked forward to giving her some peace of mind. I walked her through the steps to focus her. Taking her hand in mine, I closed my eyes. An image of the sparkling green stone formed in my head. "I see it resting at the bottom of a jewelry box," I said.

"That's where I always keep it," admitted Ms. Alma.

I waited for the image to change places, but it disappeared entirely like smoke on the wind. I blinked my eyes open. "Strange."

"What is?" Ben asked.

Unnerved, I attempted to shake it off. "Nothing. I'd like to try something else. Let's start from where you keep the jewelry box."

Ms. Alma escorted us up the stairs to a closet in her room. She took down a box, opened it, and took out another smaller box from inside like a Russian nesting doll. When we got to the wooden jewelry box, she took it out and handed it to me.

I opened it with great care and took stock of her other pieces. Simpler gems and metals rested in their place in the red velvet interior. A string of luminescent pearls lay in the back. She lifted up the first tray and pointed at an empty slot. "This is where I kept the ring all these years."

"And when was the last time you saw it?" I asked.

"Why, last week at least. I wore it with my best dress to the dance at the retirement center. Maybe someone who saw it on me wanted it," she suggested.

"You think it's been stolen, not lost?" clarified Ben.

She brushed her fingers over her other jewelry. "I can't think of another explanation. I took it off that night and placed it right back in here." She pointed at the box.

I squeezed her hand in reassurance. "Let's try another method. Ben, will you act as my guide and make sure I don't run into anything?"

With my friend's assurance, I picked up the jewelry box and gripped it tight. Closing my eyes, I summoned my magic into my core. *"Clear the fog so I can see, help me find this jewelry. The precious green so sparkling bright, from hidden dark bring to the light."*

Calling on my old tried and true ways, I waited for a glowing thread to appear. One shimmered to life and flickered with weak energy. In haste, I bound it to me and let it pull me forward.

"Where is she going?" asked Ms. Alma.

Ben shushed her, not wanting to interrupt me. I felt his hand guide me a couple of times, hopefully keeping me from bruising my head or other body parts. I took careful blind steps downstairs, still clinging to the last of the thread. It cut off and died with a suddenness that startled me. Opening my eyes, I found myself in the middle of the pantry room.

Ms. Alma stared at me with a puzzled look from the doorway. "Do you think it's in there?"

"No." I wiped the sweat from my brow. "It's not here." The chill of fear settled over me.

"You mean, it's not this room." Ben stepped inside to inspect the pantry contents.

I shook my head. "What rooms did I go into?"

"That's the thing," he stated with concern. "You went into every single room. I thought your talents were more specific."

I clutched my stomach from the void of energy as much as the pit of despair that widened inside it. "They usually are."

"What should I do now?" asked Ms. Alma.

Ben placed a sympathetic hand on my shoulder and squeezed. Turning to his client, he advised her, "I think we should go down to the warden station and file a report."

I couldn't turn and face them yet. Tears stung the corner of my eyes. "I'm sorry I couldn't help you," I croaked out.

If this had been my job, I would be a pauper. Twice now, I'd tried to work my magic and failed. Something was wrong with me, and if I couldn't fix it, then I would lose the biggest part of my identity. For all my complaints over the years, I regretted not having what I once wished away.

"Come on, Charli." Ben tugged on me. "I'll take you back to your bicycle. Call me later to let me know you're okay."

I grabbed his hand before he left. "Don't tell anybody about this," I pleaded.

"I won't." The concern in his eyes told me that he wouldn't wait long before he made that statement untrue. I had limited time to work out my issues.

I FOUND Matt rocking on my porch when I got home. The sight of my brother instantly relieved some of my doubts and concerns.

Growing up, he had been the one to help me develop my magic instead of being afraid of it. Perhaps he'd have an idea of how I could fix it now. And since I knew him better than most people, I had good blackmail material to keep him quiet about it.

"Why so glum, chum?" I asked him.

My brother rocked and frowned. "TJ won't let me help. She says I spook the horses, but I think that's just an excuse to keep me away," he complained.

The fact that he wouldn't look at me clued me in. "What did you say or do?"

"Nothing that wasn't true."

"Like what?" I pressed.

He threw his hands in the air. "I told her that she shouldn't be ridin' the horses."

"That isn't new, and the doc laid down that rule not too long ago. Why would your repeating it upset her?"

My brother grimaced. "I might have said it in a different way."

Tired of his avoidance, I smacked the back of his head. "Just spit it out."

He sighed. "I told her she was getting too big to ride."

I sucked my breath through my teeth. "Whoa, that's bad. I'm surprised you can sit down."

"I'm lucky that she doesn't use the same hex you used to

on me with too much of a free hand." He slapped my arm in retaliation. "She prefers the silent treatment, and I have to admit, her not talking to me hurts even more."

"You think you'll ever learn to keep your mouth shut?" I asked.

He rubbed the back of his neck. "I hope so, or I'm going to be a dead man with two women in the house."

My loud squeal echoed through the air. "You're having a baby girl?" I jumped up and down.

My brother's cheeks reddened. "I am. It's my luck in life to be surrounded by girls."

I smothered him with kisses and hugs until he couldn't take anymore. He fought back and captured my head in his arm, rubbing a noogie into my scalp. "Cut it out," I cried.

"Never." He rubbed with more ferocity until I pushed away from him.

I let a sparkle of energy form at my fingertips, and he held up his hands. "Hey, don't hurt the father of your future niece."

Reminded that I was going to be an aunty to a little girl, I giggled in glee, forgetting for a second about my own worries. I sat down in the chair next to him, rocking away and marveling at the twists and turns life had brought the two of us.

"How am I going to do it?" asked Matt after a few quiet moments.

"Do what?"

"Raise a daughter. I'm a boy. I know about boy things. What if I fail her?" The fear in his voice cut through me.

I patted his hand. "You won't. I promise."

"How do you know?" he asked in a quiet tone.

"Because you were a fantastic brother to me. You took my differences in stride, and instead of making me feel like a freak and an outsider, you made me stronger. And that's all you have to do." I squeezed his hand three times, my lip trembling as I reassured my brother. Blood didn't bond us, but love sure did.

"Thanks," Matt choked out. He cleared his throat. "I needed that."

My concerns could wait. Tonight, I needed to help my brother locate his courage instead of fixing my magic. "No problem. Although I'll deny saying anything nice to you to anyone else. Especially to little Charlotte, Junior."

"In your dreams, Birdy." My brother's mischievous smile returned to his face.

"Don't call me that," I insisted out of habit. "Now, go apologize to your pregnant wife."

Chapter Twelve

Nana always said that ignoring a problem means it never gets solved. I decided to prove her wrong by joining Moss and the other pixies in cleaning up one of the upstairs rooms instead of dealing with my fears about my magic. A little bit of the fairy's gray-green dust settled over me whenever she checked on my progress.

"I can do that for you, Miss Charli," she insisted.

I picked up a new pile of stuff to go through. "No, no. It's all right."

More dust spread over the papers in front of me. "If you're unhappy with our work—"

I interrupted her. "It's not that. I like cleaning," I lied. What I liked was not dwelling on my failures and having something else to focus on.

Both of us perked up at the sound of someone knocking

on my door. When I left the room, high-pitched squeals erupted. I'd bet the pixies were lodging their complaints with Moss about my presence. My roommate had been smart enough to stay out of their way.

Leaving them behind, I bounced downstairs and opened the door. "Mason," I exclaimed. "What are you doing here?"

A storm of emotions brewed inside of me. I'd wanted nothing more than to have him want me to work with him. At the same time, with my talents on the fritz, what help could I give?

"Can I help you with something?"

He looked past me. "Charli, I'm actually here to see—"

"Where are my manners," I interrupted. "Please come in. May I get you a glass of iced tea?" I rambled nonsense, realizing how hungry I was to hear more about the case or to have an excuse to spend time with him.

"No, thank you. I'm fine." He followed me inside, taking the time to examine my house. "It looks like things are coming together. It looks...nice. More like you."

"If you mean slightly dirty, a little disheveled, and barely passing, then I might agree with you. At least it's starting to feel like my home, although I'm not sure that my idea of home ever included a vampire roommate." I held back the cringe at my poor attempt at a joke.

"That's why I'm here," Mason said.

"Because you want a vampire for a roommate?"

"No. I need to question him, if you could just direct me to where he is."

"Beau," I screamed at the top of my lungs.

"What?" A muffled yell replied.

"Don't *what* me! Poof your bat behind down here. We've got company," I shouted.

Mason winced at our exchange. "Sounds like every home I've ever known," he commented.

The wooden stairs creaked under Beau's feet as he marched down to meet us. "Detective, are you here to take Miss Charli out? I heard her muttering something about a date earlier."

My hand flew up to cover the vampire's mouth. "I never said anything like that." I lowered my voice and narrowed my eyes at Beau. "You, shush."

Mason shifted in uncomfortable silence, waiting. "If you don't mind, I have some questions for you."

"For me?" my roommate and I asked at the same time.

Mason shook his head. "For you," he clarified, pointing at Beau. "Is there somewhere we can go that's more private?"

Beau scratched his almost-bald head. "Anything that needs to be said can be said in front of her. I don't require privacy in my own home."

"Then, shall we?" Mason gestured to my parlor. His formality stung, but he was on the job. Unable to help myself, I zipped to the kitchen and fixed three glasses of iced tea. Handing them around, I sat down next to Beau on the stiff couch.

Mason took out his pad and pencil. "It's my understanding that you visit the retirement home quite often. Is that true?"

"I don't think that's a secret, Detective," Beau replied.

"But you don't always sign in when you do visit," Mason observed rather than questioned.

My roommate cleared his throat. "No, not always."

"And when you do go there, who is it that you intend to see?" The detective held his pencil at the ready.

"Do you need a complete list?" Beau asked.

Mason nodded. "That would be helpful."

I attempted to hold back my surprise as my roommate revealed a long list of female names, half of whom I knew growing up. Beau paused to consider if the list was complete, and I smacked him on the arm.

"You dated all those women?" How could someone so incompetent at so many things be such a ladies' man?

"Depends on what you mean by date," he said.

"Give me your own definition, please," Mason insisted.

Beau tapped his finger against one of his fangs. "Sometimes all they want is some company. Someone to talk to or to pay attention to them. Others want a dancing partner or someone to play cards with or checkers."

"And is that all you were doing with Miss Cordelia? Playing a game of checkers in her room?" I needled.

"There are other activities that I engage in with the women when the connection is mutual. For example—"

I waved my hands, cutting him off. "I don't think we need those types of details, do we, Mason?" The two men might get their privacy if I had to listen to Beau go into any deeper descriptions.

"Maybe," Mason said. "But first, I see that you left off Eugenia Kettlefields. Was she not one of your...friends?"

Realization dawned on my roommate's face. "Oh, no. Not her. She wasn't the social type. I saw her around the place, but I wouldn't say that she had many friends there. In my estimation, she was a very lonely person."

"And you never entered her bedroom?" Mason pressed.

"No, never," answered Beau.

The detective's interrogation piqued my interest. "Why are you asking him these questions? Did you find something that puts Beau on your list of suspects?"

"Let me run things right now, Charli," Mason insisted. He produced a book from his suit pocket and placed it on the coffee table in front of us.

"That's one of our old textbooks," I observed. "Why do you have a copy of the *History of Magic?*"

"We've been collecting Mrs. Kettlefields' possessions, and cataloging them after your raid of her room. This was among them," he replied.

"I bet it's one of her teaching things she must have kept. I don't see why it would be that special." I fingered the tattered cover, remembering my time in school when my biggest worry had been memorizing the most powerful witches of the fourteenth century. As an adult, I now understood that not all of the information in the book had been completely true. As an educational tool, it was pretty useless.

"Look inside," ordered Mason.

I flipped open the cover, expecting to see a school stamp

on one side with the scrawled names of the different children who were assigned the book through the years across from the familiar title page. Instead, I found pages and pages of scribbling.

Picking the book up, I held it closer. "Is this her diary?"

"It is," admitted Mason. "You can read it," he said, granting me permission to the question I hadn't asked yet.

My eyes scanned my teacher's neat handwriting. For the most part, she wrote about how mundane her life was after being forced to quit teaching. In the beginning, she expressed her anger at her retirement, but further on, the entries confirmed what Beau had said. Without the daily contact with her pupils, Mrs. K was very forlorn.

A wave of sad sympathy washed over me. "It doesn't reveal much other than an old woman who longed for her earlier life and didn't know what to do with the rest of the time she had left."

Mason stood up and took the book out of my hand. He turned the pages until he got to where he wanted and handed it back to me, pointing where I should start.

The tone of her words changed rapidly. Instead of bitter complaints, her words expressed joy and elation.

"It has been so long since I have felt this alive. Not since the first time and seeing my words come to life on the stage by my dear students. It's as if my life has been lived in darkness and somebody has switched on the lights."

I turned the page. The next few entries were the same, expressing her newfound happiness. I started to skip and scan her words until I noticed an even more significant change. Hasty scribbles replaced the careful script.

A shaky hand wrote the words. *"The thing I feared most is coming true. My mind is slipping, much like my dear departed mother's. I am finding I have patches of time gone. Memories that aren't there. Holes in my narrative. Perhaps I should tell someone, but I don't want to be taken away. Mother was taken, and she was never the same."*

I turned the page. *"I have misplaced the brooch I hold so dear. Its value may not be high to others, but my retirement gift holds a priceless value for me. Much like some of my memories, I cannot seem to find it."*

The next entry disturbed me more. *"There are thoughts in my head that I do not know if they are mine or someone else's. I am unsettled most of the time. I find the most comfort in my normal routine of life, and still crave those stolen moments where I am shown how I can be truly free."*

"I don't know if I want to finish this," I admitted. It was one thing to suspect that someone's sanity was spiraling into an abyss but a whole other thing to witness it in her writing.

"Skip to the last entry," Mason said.

I turned to the final page with cursive on it. *"He tells me that I will know when the time has come to speak my mind. A part of me questions his reasons, but then another part of me desires to make him happy. I am being torn in two, and am not sure what will become of me."*

"*Him*," I emphasized. "That's why you're questioning Beau."

"I swear to you, I never spent time with Mrs. Kettlefields." My roommate shifted in discomfort next to me. "If you need confirmation of that, then I suggest gathering the testimonies of those women. But I would prefer if you did it one at a time and not all at once, if you don't mind."

Mason made some notes. "I may have to do that, and I make no guarantees. For now, I suggest you cease-and-desist any nighttime visits there. I've already started asking some questions, and you may find your welcome mat taken away for the moment."

"I understand," Beau grumbled. He stood up and stomped his way back upstairs.

Left alone with Mason, too many questions bubbled to the surface. "I think you can rule out suicide."

"That was unlikely anyway, considering that her official death was lack of oxygen from being choked. Still, it does show that her mind was not quite right," he replied.

My pulse quickened. "Which might explain her outburst during the first election event—"

"—but not why she was killed," finished Mason.

Our ideas flowed so well together. Almost like before, when we put together the pieces of Tipper's demise, and I grabbed hold of the moment, not wanting to let go.

"About that brooch," Mason said. "If you have the time, would you be willing to come with me and help search for it?"

The adrenaline of excitement rushed through me. "Of course," I declared without thinking. When my brain caught up, I winced. "Except..." With my magic not working quite right, was it worth making the attempt only to fail?

I picked up the glasses to take to the kitchen. "By the way, did Ms. Alma ever file a report about her missing ring?"

Confusion settled on his brow. "I don't know. I'll have to check on that when I go back to the station. Or you could come back with me, and we can check together before you help me find the missing piece of jewelry."

The grandfather clock in the foyer chimed the hour, and I panicked. "Uh, I can't right now." I stood up in haste and ushered Mason toward the door. "Maybe later."

Why hadn't I been paying attention to the time? Of course, it wouldn't matter much if it weren't Mason still standing in my house on any normal day, which today definitely was not.

The detective chuckled at my insistence. "I'm entirely capable of leaving on my own, Charli." He didn't seem to appreciate my hands on his back, pushing. "What's the rush? Is Beau right? Do you have a date?"

I grunted in exasperation. "No, it's not a date."

"Yes, it is." Dash's deep voice countered my protest. He peered over Mason's shoulder at me. "And you're running late."

The detective's face dropped, and he shook it off. With his cool mask of professionalism back in place, he turned to greet the shifter. "Dash." He stuck out his hand to shake.

"Mason," Dash replied. The wolf shifter opened the screen door wide and moved to let the detective walk by.

"Thank you for your assistance," Mason said to me over his shoulder.

"Am I interrupting something?" Dash asked.

"We're done here." Mason left without looking back.

A butter knife couldn't cut the tension in the air. The clock ticked every tense second.

Dash regarded me with wary eyes. "If you don't want to go, I won't be upset." The glare in his eyes told a different story.

"Just give me a quick second, and I'll be ready for our," I paused. "Lunch... thing... picnic."

"Then I'll wait right here to take you to our lunch, thing, picnic," Dash teased. "But hurry up because I'm hungry." His eyes flashed, and, I swear, he licked his fangs.

Chapter Thirteen

The twisting branches of the Founders' tree dripped with lush strands of Spanish moss. Its leafy canopy offered shade from the hot sun. It surprised me they had picked this location for our lunch, but the low-hanging branches that dipped into and out of the ground did provide a decent place to sit.

Blythe busied herself arranging the food on a blanket in front of us, the contents so numerous that she almost ran out of room. She hummed out of tune under her breath. She *never* hummed.

Damien watched with fascination. "I must admit, I do not recall partaking in a picnic that was so bounteous. Explain to me what we have."

Blythe pointed at her contributions. "This one is coleslaw,

which is grated cabbage. I also fixed macaroni salad and stole some of Mr. Steve's potato salad as well."

The vampire examined each one. "I find it fascinating that you use that word, and yet, I see no green in those dishes."

My friend held up a finger. "That's why I made an actual *salad* salad as well."

Damien laughed with enthusiasm, and Dash smiled. I did my best not to mock my friend for her bubbly joke, trying to remind myself that everyone deserved a chance at whatever happiness they found. Even if it changed their personalities.

The vampire took a sip of his drink and screwed up his face. "I am not sure I will ever get used to that amount of sugar nor having my teeth cold."

"I thought you were from London," Dash remarked. "Isn't that place full tea drinkers?"

Damien set his cup down, balancing it on the ground. "Yes, of course. But we prefer that it is hot, and usually take either milk or lemon with it depending on what type of tea it is. My particular favorite is the Oolong blend they serve at The Savoy. It is the Queen's favorite, you know. What kind do you use to make this concoction?"

"The kind that comes in a bag," I answered.

Blythe shot me a look of warning at my sarcastic remark before continuing. "Dash here has provided us with our main course, fried chicken." She unfolded the red-and-white checkered towel covering the delectable golden brown treat.

"You made it?" I asked.

Dash lifted his finger to my chin and closed my mouth.

"Don't be so surprised. I have many talents you don't know about." He placed a couple of pieces on a plate next to the other food he'd already scooped out and handed it to me.

"And many secrets," I added.

"But not as many as I used to keep from you," he replied in a low voice.

I stared at his lips. "I kind of like a man who can cook."

"Good. Because I like a girl who can bake. I can't wait to get a piece of your pie." He wiggled his eyebrows at me, and the heat between us almost matched the midday temperature.

I shoved him in play to break the tension.

"Try it," he insisted with enthusiasm and little bit of nerves, waiting for me to taste his contribution.

I sank my teeth into the slightly warm chicken leg. The crust crackled and flaked in my mouth with good crunch. The meat tasted tender and juicy, almost rivaling my Nana's recipe. "Holy unicorn horn, so good," I managed through my full mouth.

Blythe nodded in agreement. "You've got a nice scald on it. Did you brine the meat first?"

"Of course." Dash chewed off a piece. "That's my secret."

"Buttermilk?" I asked, taking another large bite.

He shook his head. "Nope. I might as well tell you because you'll never guess. It's sweet tea."

"Really? Steve uses buttermilk at the cafe," Blythe said.

The shifter swallowed. "My mother didn't always have access to buttermilk. But there was always sweet tea in the house growing up."

"I take it back. Maybe your sweet tea concoction does have its place. This is indeed delicious." The vampire picked up a thigh with his fingers, unable to hide his discomfort at our lack of utensils.

Curling his upper lip, he took the teeniest bite I'd ever seen with his non-fanged teeth. "Mmm," he emitted, chewing. "Truly delicious." It didn't escape my notice that he did not partake of much of the food, which made me question why we were all here in the first place.

Blythe wiped her mouth with a napkin. "Did you hear that Horatio has officially dropped out of the election?"

The information didn't surprise me after my talk with Juniper, but disappointment still filled my chest. "It really is too bad that DK has given Linsey a full-time reporter's job. She seems to walk a fine line between facts and conjecture."

"Scandal remains one of the world's best currencies," commented Damien. "It sells newspapers and generates money as well as gossip. It can take a person from obscurity and raise them into infamy or sink an entire nation."

"Is that what you found in your travels?" I asked, my cold gaze landing on the vampire's, trying to figure him out.

"One of many things," replied Damien, not backing down from my visual challenge.

"Let's not talk politics, guys," insisted Blythe.

The four of us settled into quiet eating. Well, three of us. Damien continued to pick at the food on his plate rather than indulge. I got lost in my thoughts, going over Mrs. K's diary entries in my head. The poor woman had been so lonely, and not one of her former students came by to visit. We'd all mocked her and locked her away in our memory, assigning her the role of a ridiculous caricature of who she really was. Only the mysterious *he* had made an attempt to connect with her, and even that person seemed questionable.

When I remembered that Mason wanted me to help find her missing brooch, I stopped eating, my stomach turning a bit with worry.

Dash kicked my shin, interrupting my thoughts.

"What?" I rubbed the spot.

Blythe stared daggers at me. "You didn't answer Damien's question."

"Ask me again," I insisted, giving him my full attention.

My friend repeated the vampire's words with slow deliberation. "He wants to know if you've lived here all your life."

"Oh. Yes, for the most part, Honeysuckle was and still is my home, although I don't know if Blythe told you about my year spent away. But I'm honestly glad to be back." There. Now, she couldn't complain that I wasn't taking part in the conversation.

"And your brother works with the town's wardens?" asked Damien, barely waiting for my reply before adding, "And with the last name of Goodwin, may I presume that you are related to the honorable woman who sits in the high seat on the town council?"

"It seems you've done your homework." If the man wanted

to start a better conversation, he needed to ask me more than yes or no questions.

"Tell him what it's like being a member of one the founding families, Charli." Blythe lifted her eyebrows at me, her unspoken irritation clear as day.

"It's...fine?" What could I really say?

Dash leaned over to me and whispered in my ear. "Be nice."

I shrugged him off and added, "It means my grandmother tends to be pretty busy all year-round." There. Damien could chew on that since he wasn't chewing on anything else.

"You could tell him about your family's participation in things like the founding ceremony." My friend turned to Damien. "Only the founding family members know what treasures are buried underneath this tree."

I dropped my cup, and ice-cold sweet tea spilled all over me. "Blythe," I exclaimed.

"What?" she snapped back. "He's been showing an interest in our town history. And since he's thinking of putting down roots here, I don't see the harm in him knowing about stuff like that."

"But you're not supposed to say anything about the specifics. If he stays, he'll find out on his own." I batted Dash's hand away from mopping up the liquid with a napkin, wiping it overly close to my chest.

Blythe set her plate down and stood up, towering over me. "What's your problem, Charli?"

"What's yours?" I returned, struggling to stand so I could face her.

"He has been nothing but nice, and you can't summon up the energy to engage in regular conversation." She placed her hand on her hip.

"And you said you would never let a man turn you into a fool." I countered. "You never giggle or hum."

She stepped closer to me and narrowed her eyes. "The only foolish thing I've done is invited you here today."

"I didn't want to come anyway," I yelled.

"Then leave," she demanded.

Before I could reply, Dash pulled me by my arm until we stood a few feet away. I kept my eyes on Damien who comforted Blythe with his arms around her.

"What is wrong with you?" Dash repeated with a bit of a snarl in his tone.

Fed up with trying to ignore my gut, I bellowed the truth. "I don't like him."

The shifter didn't let me off that easy. "What don't you like?"

"There's something about him." No matter how hard I tried, I couldn't shake that nagging feeling inside. "He makes me uneasy."

A shadow crossed Dash's face. "Because he's hogging your friend's attention? Or because he's not like you guys?"

I pointed at Damien. "But he's not. Look at him. The guy is wearing a suit on a picnic. Clearly, he's used to being around others, and doesn't quite fit in here."

"You mean like I didn't," Dash countered in a lower voice.

My eyes snapped away from Blythe and landed on him. "I didn't say that."

"But you are implying it," he challenged. "Just because he doesn't fit in your witch world doesn't mean he should be discounted."

"So now you're coming to his defense? I thought wolves and vampires didn't get along." My bratty statement landed the blow I desired.

Dash winced. "That's werewolves, and that's only in fiction."

I sucked in a breath, knowing I'd crossed a line. "Dash, I didn't mean it."

"Yes, you did."

My head spun with everything going on. The bit of lunch I'd eaten threatened to come back up. "I've got to go." Hopping on my bike, I ran away from yet another problem. Dash's question gnawed on me as I rode away.

What *was* wrong with me?

Chapter Fourteen

✣

I must have circled the streets surrounding the warden station more than ten times, unable to decide whether or not to go in or go home. After another circuit around, Zeke stood in front of my path, blocking me from riding past the station. I braked hard to avoid hitting him.

He held onto my handlebars. "Miss Charli, your brother sent me out here to find out why you keep passing by. He suggested that you either come in or go home. Except...he didn't say it in such a nice way."

"Let me guess. He said something about using the bathroom or not, right?" I smirked.

Zeke avoided my devious glance. "Something like that, miss."

I put the young warden out of his misery. "Tell my brother

I'll stop in to see him in a few." Parking my bike in the lot, I followed Zeke inside.

Mason stood by the front desk. "And how was your lunch date?" he mocked.

"Don't ask," I warned.

The detective acted interested. "That good?"

"Or that bad." He didn't need the specifics, but he could wipe that smug satisfaction off his face anytime now.

"Come to my office," he requested.

Once inside, Mason closed the door behind me. He pointed to a box on his desk. "I've brought in some of her things that seemed more personal to her."

I stood on my tiptoes to try and catch a glimpse of what things he'd chosen. "Why?"

"I thought that's how it worked. If you couldn't hold the person's hand, you could use something of value to them to help find whatever it is you're searching for." The detective proved his skills in observation, knowing my exact methods.

My hands trembled, and I squeezed them into fists. Twice now, I'd tried and failed. If I attempted to help Mason and nothing happened, I didn't think I could face his disappointment in me.

"I don't know if now is a good time. Maybe we should try later," I managed. With fast feet, I moved to the door, turning the knob.

Mason took long strides to catch up and slammed the door shut with his hand, trapping me inside. "Charli, I don't get it. You made it clear that you wanted to work with me, but as soon as I ask for your help, you refuse? Tell me what it is you *do* want."

I started to explain to him the reason I needed to leave had more to do with me than him, but he didn't give me a chance to respond.

He leaned against the door, trapping me with his body. "I don't know what you want me to say. I guess I felt like you see me differently after that thing with Skeeter. I know that my actions weren't exactly honorable." He cast his eyes to the floor, swallowing hard.

Nana was right, not that she didn't have a gold medal in that. Still, my heart melted a bit at his embarrassment. "Mason, everyone in there was under the influence. Remember how no one was arrested? That's because my grandmother was right when she said that none of you could be held responsible for your actions. All this time you avoided me because you thought I would think less of you?"

He closed the distance between us, and I could detect a slight whiff of soap and cologne from his skin. "No. I was afraid you would see too much." Mason stood in front of me stripped bare of any pretense. The truth radiated off of him, raw and rare. Instead of keeping me at arm's length, he was drawing me in as close as I'd ever been. His trust and vulnerability shattered me, and I couldn't stop the tears from streaming down my cheeks.

The detective's face softened. "I didn't mean to make you cry."

I waved my hand in protest, unable to speak for fear that a sob would rack my body.

He didn't hesitate or leave. Instead, he wrapped his arms around my body and pulled me in tight. There was no demand from his touch other than for me to take the comfort that he gave freely. I soaked it all up, snotting into his shoulder until my body stopped shaking and the flood of emotions evened out.

His whispers of assurances ceased, and he rubbed my back in slower circles. The heat from his body penetrated mine, and I became intensely aware of his touch. With a sniff, I extracted myself from his embrace. Like a true gentleman, he offered me a tissue from a box on his desk. It took a few deep breaths for me to compose myself before I could give a full explanation.

"My magic isn't working," I admitted in shame.

My effort to cut to the chase caught him off guard. "I don't understand."

"That night with Raif's dog, when you brought me to him to help. When I tried to use my magic to find his pug, nothing happened."

Mason shook his head. "You mean you were interrupted. I remember that you tried, but your brother brought Mrs. K before anything happened."

The detective's point of view was a little skewed. I wished it were true, but I needed him to hear the truth. "No. I took Raif's hand, and when I focused my magic, nothing appeared for me. Literally, nothing. Normally, I can connect to whatever it is I'm searching for at least a little. But with Raif, it was all one big blank."

Mason rubbed his chin, scratching his afternoon stubble. "Maybe that's his fault. He wasn't exactly enthusiastic to have you help in the first place."

"Yeah, but I think his desire to find his beloved dog would overrule any personal feelings he has for me." I took a deep breath and steadied myself to continue. "But that's not the only time."

I described my experience with Ben and Ms. Alma's ring. "Again, I've never had it go so wrong. I've worked with a loose connection before, and have managed to make it work. Frosted fairy wings, searching for things like that is child's play for me. I mean, when I was a child, I could do better. I have no idea why I can't wield my magic, and if I can't anymore, then I'll be nothing." The tears started all over again, and I grabbed more tissues from the box.

Mason leaned on the edge of his desk, giving me the space to cry. When the sniffles stopped, he spoke in a gentle voice, "You're being ridiculous."

"No, I'm not." I sounded like a petulant child.

"You are. You've grown up in a world that hammered into you that your talents made you special. Either you were bullied because you were different or you were told how rare you really were. You've gotten used to the attention that your magic brings to you." He touched my arm. "But you have no idea what it is that makes you special."

He ran his hand down my skin and grasped both of my

hands in his. "You, Charlotte Goodwin, have more strength and backbone than one hundred people I've known. You stand up for what you believe in without a care for the consequences. You are loyal to a fault, and you love hard."

Unable to bear the weight of his words, I glanced down. He let go of one of my hands and cupped my chin, lifting my head to face him. "The biggest magic you wield is how, even though you can be infuriatingly stubborn at times, you make those around you care about you. More than maybe they should." His thumb brushed my cheek. "It's a spell that's hard to break," he said in almost a whisper.

A knock on the door broke the heated bubble around us, and Zeke entered the office without waiting for a response. I squeaked and jumped away from Mason, allowing him to deal with warden business. When he finished, he shut the door again but kept his distance for me.

"Have you told anybody about your problem? Seen the doc?" he asked.

Disappointment seeped into my spirit at the return of the professional warden. "It's not something I want to get around."

"Especially to your family, I would bet."

I snapped to attention. "You aren't going to tell my brother, are you?"

He crossed his arms over his chest. "I don't know yet. I reserve the right if I think you're at the point where you can't handle things yourself. But Charli, you're talking about only two instances. Any others?"

"No," I admitted. "I've been too afraid to try."

He looked at the box on his desk and back at me. "Listen, I want to help, and I will. But I'm not going to push you. If you want to take a day to decide, then I guess that will be fine. But if you change your mind, and I can't lie, I hope you do, then call me." Mason pulled out a spell phone from his jacket and showed it to me.

"Where did you get that?" I asked.

"Lee gave it to Big Willie, but the sheriff didn't want to take the time to mess with it." He flipped the phone open, and with a press of a button, the one in my pocket buzzed and emitted that annoyingly loud ring I hadn't taken the time to change yet. "And now you have my number. Use it," he insisted.

"I will." I glanced at him with suspicion. "Why are you letting me off so easy?"

He put his spell phone back in his pocket. "Because you don't need me pushing you. And I'm pretty sure you'll call me."

His satisfied grin amused me. "You're sure of yourself."

Opening the door, he ushered me out. "No. I'm certain of your inability to stay away. Talk to you later." He huffed out a breath when I smacked him in his stomach as I passed.

I almost made it out of the station when Matt caught me. "Hey, Birdy. Everything good?"

For some reason, my short time with the detective had been a salve to my emotional wounds. "Don't call me that. And yeah, I think it will be."

"Good." My brother ruffled my hair. "Then maybe you'll stop acting nuts, circling the station, and making everyone question your sanity. By the way, Nana's lookin' for you. She wants you to stop by her house before you go home."

"Thanks." Checking to see if anyone was watching, I punched him in the arm.

"Ow, what was that for?" He rubbed at the spot.

"For being my concerned big brother."

"You know I could put you in a holding cell for assaulting a warden," Matt warned.

I bounced my way to the door. "You could, but you won't," I sang out to him, waving.

Chapter Fifteen

Nana waited for me on her porch. I would never figure out how that woman always knew things.

"I have something for you," she said when I joined her.

"Is it more food that you've cooked?" I followed her inside, almost tripping over a furry orange and gray mass in the middle of the floor. Peaches liked to go between the two houses, somehow needing to visit her friend Loki almost as much as wanting to live with me. Since she was almost out of kittenhood, I didn't mind that she had her own life.

Nana called out to me, and I found her in the kitchen. Instead of something yummy, she handed me a glass with dirty gray sludge in it. "Drink it down," she ordered.

I'd had my fill of her concoction when she was trying to

save me from Uncle Tipper's death curse. Enough for three lifetimes. "Why do I have to drink that?" I asked.

Nana didn't give me a reason. "I don't have time to argue, Charli. I've got to get ready to go in and help set up for the night's debate at the town hall. So why don't we jump from you whinin' about it to you drinkin' it."

"But there's nothing wrong with me," I protested.

My grandmother gave me her patented steely glare. "You've got exactly ten seconds, young lady."

The adult in me wanted to slam the glass down and refuse, but the child in me remembered what happened when she ran out of numbers. Pinching my nose, I lifted the glass to my lips and swallowed as fast as possible. It still tasted like mud and dirt or exactly what I imagined unicorn manure would be like. In other words, the exact opposite of sweet tea. I got halfway finished and stopped to take a gulp of air.

"Finish it all up." Nana tapped the watch on her wrist.

With a moan, I obeyed, downing the entire contents in record time. I wiped my lips with the back of my hand and shuddered. "How did you know?" I asked.

"You know better than to ask me that. Have you seen my lucky necklace anywhere?" she asked, pushing past me and rushing up the stairs.

I followed behind, puzzled. "No, but I haven't been here that much."

I spotted Moss coming out of my old bedroom and greeted her. My presence surprised the small fairy, and her wings quivered, gray-green dust falling on the floor.

With a sour face, she floated down and cleaned up her mess. "I left a pile of papers for you to go through on the coffee table in your parlor, Miss Charli," she said while cleaning.

"Thank you, Moss." I listened to my grandmother rattling around in her room. She emerged looking harrowed and anxious.

"Well, I can't find it anywhere." She stomped down the stairs, and I followed in her wake.

"Nana, slow down."

My grandmother stopped in her tracks. Turning around, she gripped both my hands. "The debate tonight has to go well. Everything about the election is hanging by a thread. If anything else goes wrong, who knows how the town will react? Big Willie tells me they're no closer to solving Mrs. K's death."

I hugged my grandmother tight. "That's a lot of weight on your shoulders. There are a lot more people in this town that you can rely on. You don't have to take on the problems all by yourself."

For once, I provided the stable foundation for my grandmother to lean on. Wrapping my arms around her, I forced her to take a timeout. She slumped into my embrace and gave in.

"You have grown wise in your old age," she joked, patting my back and letting me go.

"I had a good role model," I said, smoothing out a strand of her hair. "I don't think a hug will be seen as the solution to world peace, but it's about all I can offer you."

"I don't know," chortled my grandmother. "We have to get all the world leaders, both human and magical, in the same room and try it before we could test that statement." She cupped my cheek and gazed at me with love. "I'm sorry I haven't been here for you lately. You know you can tell me anything, right?"

I nodded. "There's nothing to tell," I assured her, wanting to keep my troubles away from her.

She kissed my forehead. "Good. So then it doesn't matter whether or not you drank my stuff or whether you're telling me the truth. It won't hurt you, and if you need it, it'll help."

I rubbed my stomach and wrinkled my nose. "My taste buds disagree. I'll see you at the debates tonight. Do you want me to lock up the house when I leave?"

"No," Nana said through the screen door. "Juniper's here with her crew. She'll finish up and fix everything. Oh, and there's a pineapple upside down cake in the refrigerator if you want to take it home with you."

"Still cooking away your troubles?" I called out to her.

My grandmother waved at me as she left. "It's medicine for the soul."

"Better than gray sludge," I teased. Picking up my sassy little orange cat, who stretched in front of me and wrapped herself around my ankles, I listened to her incessant meows. "What's that? You want to go home with me?"

She purred in my hands, and I cuddled her little body next to my ear, listening to the rolling sound. "Okay, we'll go home in a second. I want to go check something in my room," I told Peaches, setting her down.

Bounding up the stairs and skipping the noisy ones, I made my way to my old room. Standing in the doorway, I caught a glimpse of something shiny dangling from Juniper's hand. "Good luck tonight at the debate," I said, startling the fairy.

Whatever she held clattered to the floor. She zipped down and picked it up. "I-I f-f-found this," she defended, holding it out to me.

I opened up my hand and received what I identified as Nana's lucky necklace. "Thanks."

Juniper's eyes widened, and her wings trembled. "You're w-w-welcome," she stammered.

A heavy weight anchored my heart. Why had she been holding my grandmother's necklace? More importantly, why did she look like a cornered animal? "Is everything okay?" I asked.

"Y-y-yes," she stuttered. "It's just nerves." She coughed. "And now that Horatio is no longer running, I will be representing both of our issues. It's a lot to take on." She dipped in the air as if her worries physically weighed her down.

"If it's too much, I'm sure Horatio would support you if you wanted to drop out," I said.

"Oh no," she gasped in her tiny voice. "I could never do that to him. I would do anything to keep him from being disappointed." Juniper frowned in determination when she said that last sentence.

"Then I hope everything goes well for you tonight. I'll be cheering you on." My sincere sentiments didn't lessen my growing suspicions.

She brightened at my good wishes and then drooped again as she gazed at the chain of the necklace falling through my fingers. "Thank you," she muttered almost too quiet to be heard. "I should help finish the job so I can spend the rest of the afternoon preparing." The fairy fluttered away, leaving me with my concern.

I forgot what I'd come in to look for as I pondered if what I'd just witnessed meant what I thought it did. Had I caught my friend in the middle of taking one of my grandmother's prized possessions or was she being a conscientious cleaner, finding the necklace in some odd spot? And why was she in my old room?

If I wanted answers, now was the best time to confront her, but my doubt stopped me. If she were my friend, didn't I trust her? If I made accusations and was wrong, I could ruin our relationship. The poor tiny being had enough on her plate with tonight's event. For now, I didn't need to add to her worries.

I pocketed Nana's necklace, determined to give it to her before the debates started. Walking back downstairs, I headed to the kitchen. Instead of taking the cake home with me, I pulled it out and cut a slice, eating it one slow bite at a time, waiting for the fairies to finish.

After two slices, I surprised Juniper again when she popped in. "Oh, Charli, you scared me. I was getting ready to close everything up and didn't know you were still here."

I pointed at the plate. "Couldn't pass up Nana's upside down pineapple cake. Do you want to take some home to Horatio?" I asked.

She shook her head. "No, thanks. I'll see you later." With the flapping of wings, she left.

Putting the cake back in the fridge, I took careful steps to the front door and made sure Juniper and Moss were gone. Before I left the house, I visited every single room and examined as many nooks and crannies as I could. I was looking for everything and hoping I found nothing.

Without my grandmother's confirmation, I couldn't be sure, but for the most part, I didn't see anything out of place or missing. A small bit of relief eased my doubts about my friend.

Picking up my cat, I closed up the house and retrieved my bike. Peaches hopped into her normal spot in the front basket.

After today's events, I deserved a much-needed nap. The motorcycle parked outside my house and the muscled bearded man rocking on my front porch stood in my way. Unfortunately, I couldn't bypass him and bound inside like my kitty.

"I'm sorry I was such a witch to you today, okay?" I said, unwilling to play any games.

"Thank you," Dash accepted in his gruff voice. "Me, too."

Apologies traded, I expected him to leave. When he didn't, the awkward silence grew between us. I blew out a breath. "And?" I pushed.

He picked up a helmet from beside him and pushed himself up from the rocking chair. "And I thought maybe I could make it up to you by taking you for a ride."

I'd fantasized about riding behind the wolf shifter more than once with my arms wrapped around his waist, leaning into his solid back. And I missed the speed of a real bike. Taking the helmet from him, I planted it on my head in response.

Dash chuckled but didn't say anything else. We approached his motorcycle, and he straddled it, holding it steady for me to hop on. He took the helmet draped over the handlebar and secured it on his head.

"Hold on tight," he instructed.

My hands detected the ridges of his muscular abs through his shirt. He squirmed under my touch. "Don't tell me you're ticklish," I giggled.

"Just another secret revealed." With a flick of a switch and a kick, he started the motor. The bike vibrated beneath me, and I tightened my grip.

He took us to the road with slow care, but as soon as we hit the pavement, he revved the engine and took off. The wind whipped around us, and the rumble of the bike filled my ears. It had been a long time since I reveled in that sound of freedom. I let out a thunderous war whoop, and Dash shifted gears.

"Let 'er rip," I yelled.

We traversed the edges of town away from any traffic. There weren't many opportunities to fly, but speed wasn't the whole point. My stomach clenched in excitement, and I couldn't suppress the effervescent giggles that kept bubbling out of me.

Sunlight dappled through the trees when we turned down my favorite road. Live oaks lined either side and Spanish moss hung down, creating a canopy effect. Finding a long straightaway, Dash hit the gas. I trusted him with my life, knowing he would never let anything happen to it whether on the back of a motorcycle or not.

The gatehouse loomed closer and closer, and the wolf shifter slowed down. He pulled off to the side of the road before we reached the edge of Honeysuckle, and he let the bike idle.

Taking off his helmet, he checked on me. "You doing okay? I can feel you laughing."

"I'm absolutely perfect." My worries had been left behind in the wind.

His own chuckle vibrated under my palms. "Good. I know we've got the debates tonight, so I have to take you home."

"As long as you take the long way back." I bit my lip and batted my eyelashes.

He revved his bike to life and shouted, "As you wish." His genuine smile should be listed as an eighth deadly sin.

Turning us around, he waited for me to squeeze him tight one more time. When we raced back toward town, I swore I heard him howl with happiness.

Chapter Sixteen

The bells on the door of Sweet Tooths Bakery tinkled when Lee led Ben and me inside. A long line of people waited to buy out the rest of the baked goods from the former tooth fairies who buzzed about behind the counter filling orders. Discussions about the night's debate peppered the air, and I listened in to catch anything alarming.

Alison Kate approached us and kissed Lee on the cheek. "Sprinkle and Twinkle said we could all stay after they close up. If you want to wait inside, I think Lily and Lavender are seated over there." She pointed to a far corner.

"Excuse me, Miss Charli." A gentle hand pushed on my back to move me out of the doorway.

"Henry, I'm surprised you're not at the cafe with Flint," I chastised the elder jokester.

He nodded at the display case. "If you want pie, you go to the cafe. But if you want a slice of red velvet, you have to come here. Sassy may be good with her pie crusts, but she has a devil of a time with her cakes."

"I'll go grab you a slice before they're all gone, Mr. Henry." Alison Kate disappeared through the noisy crowd.

"Much obliged," the older gentleman called out to her. He touched my arm. "It's a flyin' shame that there troll dropped out. If anyone coulda given the vampire a verbal whoopin', it was him. That Horace was a longshot-and-a-half, and his timid giddy girlfriend isn't going to get anywhere even with the troll coaching her. It may be a tight race between the one with a pointed hat versus the one with pointy teeth." He tapped his own enamel in his mouth for emphasis.

"Horatio. That's the name of the troll," corrected Lee. He left with Ben to join the cousins at their table.

"Whatever his name. I don't think he'd hurt a fly. A fella who can talk like that doesn't need to use his fists." Henry accepted a small white box from Alison Kate and handed her some money. "Keep the change. Y'all have a good night. I'm gonna enjoy givin' Sassy some grief by eatin' this at the cafe."

As the baked goods disappeared, so did the number of people until Twinkle locked the doors. Alison Kate got up from the table to help her bosses clean up and prep for the next day. I stared at the empty space next to me where Blythe usually sat. She had gleefully joined Damien afterward to celebrate with Raif's team. It felt like a betrayal of everything I ever knew about her, even up to a few days ago.

"Does it bother anyone else that Blythe isn't here?" I asked the table at large.

"She's having fun with her new crush. I don't see anything wrong with that." A new recruit to love, Lily touched Ben's hand.

"It just feels unnatural that she's hanging out with Raif, my aunt, and the Hawthornes." That would include my cousin and Tucker as well. "It's like she's switched teams."

Lavender clicked her tongue at me. "It's not an us versus them scenario. You used to hang out with most of those people before."

"I used to be engaged to Tucker. I find myself much happier in my present company," I declared, smiling at my friends. "All except Lee who can't be bothered to participate in the conversation because he's too busy with his nose buried in his spell phone working on something with his tongue sticking out. And I bet he smells and picks his nose and farts rainbows like a unicorn."

Without looking up from his device, Lee snorted. "I heard all of that. I'm checking to make sure my latest update went through before I send it to all of you. And I definitely don't fart rainbows."

Finishing off the homemade moon pie on my plate, I licked my fingers clean of any chocolate and marshmallowy sweetness. "I thought Flint spoke well tonight."

Ben leaned back in his chair and draped his arm around the back of Lily's. "He did, but Raif had a stronger response for most of the issues. I thought he was slightly out of line when he somehow managed to connect the death of Mrs. K to Horatio whenever Juniper spoke."

"It was completely unnecessary bullying," agreed Lily.

Lavender took a sip from her drink. "That poor fairy looked like she could burst into tears at any moment, she was so nervous."

"Hey, what did her aura look like?" I asked. "Does anxiety show up as a color? Or how about having a massive ego like Raif?"

"I'll bet being pompous has to have a really ugly color. Like puce. Pompous puce. Wait, is puce a bad color?" Lily asked.

Ben squeezed her hand in his. "It's more of a grayish purple-brown color."

"Sounds about like unicorn manure. That could work," I said, wrinkling my nose at the idea. "So how about it, Lav?"

My sensitive friend shrugged. "I don't know. I can't read the auras of fairies or vampires. I have to rely on my sense of their emotions when I'm with them in person."

Her revelation shocked me. "Really? I never knew that. Is it because whatever magic they possess is different from ours?"

"Maybe. Or maybe they have a way of blocking me," Lavender suggested.

Since we all grew up in a town with a mix of different magical beings, it didn't come naturally to see anyone as that different from me other than maybe the obvious things like size. The whole point of our little home in the Southern sticks was to give a safe place for anyone who didn't fit in anywhere else. Yes, we started with witches, but our community grew to have a myriad of lives living together.

"Is it just Raif you can't read or all vampires?" Thoughts of trying to dig up more on Damien formed in my devious brain.

"All of them," admitted Lavender. "I think because, you know, they're living but they're not at the same time."

"So that rules out mummies," contributed Lee without looking up.

"And zombies," I pointed out, unable not to chuckle.

Alison Kate took the chair from beside me and dragged it to sit next to her boyfriend. "Who's a zombie?"

Lee finally stopped obsessing over his device. "Nobody, sweetums. Okay, everybody take your phones out. The updates should have gone through by now."

We obeyed and listened to him give overly elaborate descriptions on how his spellwork interacted with the human technology. Weaved between his excited explanations were detailed instructions on how we could now send texts back and forth to each other. He got stopped several times and started over again from the beginning to our major frustration.

I waved my hands in front of me. "Whoa. I think you're making this too difficult. We don't have to know *why* it works, just that it does. If I'm understanding you, we press this button," I showed him which one, "and speak. The text will show up on the screen. Like so."

Pushing the button, I dictated, "Lee is a gigantic, glasses-wearing nerd of a witch." The words showed up on my phone. After selecting his name from my contacts, I finished the action.

His phone pinged, and he showed us his received text. "You can also use the keypad numbers like Charli says they used to, but it takes longer. And, by the way, I'm proud of my geeky magical status." He pushed his glasses up his nose and received a kiss from Alison Kate in victory. "Also, if you press the Menu button and hold it down for more than five seconds, an alert will be sent to the warden station. I'm still working on the spell to allow them to locate you if you activate the emergency function."

We clapped with enthusiasm, declaring our friend a genius. "You're going to make a lot of money in magical communities," I declared.

"Me and Dash. Part of the idea belongs to him. We have an agreement." Lee returned to messing with his phone.

"Where is the wolf shifter tonight? I thought he was going to join us." He'd sat next to me during the debates, adding his own commentary throughout and trying to make me snort out loud. I couldn't kick the feeling that I wanted to ask him to take me for a ride again.

Lee looked up and checked outside the bakery's window. "I don't know. I thought he was coming, but when we were heading this way, he said he wanted to stop by Lucky's bar for a couple of minutes. I'll be honest, I almost joined him."

Alison Kate hooked her arm through his and leaned her

head on his shoulder. "But you thought better of it and came in to support me and my shop."

He kissed the top of her head. "That's right, my hot little honey bunny with honeysuckle icing." Lee flipped us off after the rest of us groaned and threw our napkins at the two of them.

Standing up, I stretched. "I think I'll go find Dash. Ben, can I have a quick word with you?" I pulled him to his feet and dragged him with me away from the others. Lowering my voice, I interrogated him. "What did you tell my grandmother?"

A sheepish look shadowed his face. "What did she tell you that I told her?"

I placed a hand on my hip. "Don't play advocate with me and redirect *my* question with another question. Did you tell her about my problems?"

Ben squinted. "N-o-t exactly," he dragged out. "But the woman has a way of getting information out of you. She'd have made a fantastic advocate."

I snorted. "Tell me about it. So you didn't give her any specifics?"

"Uh-uh." My legal friend shook his head. "Why?"

I grabbed him by his shirt and pulled him closer. "Because I had to drink an entire tall glass of that nasty, disgusting, revolting sludge. All because of *you*."

Lily noticed my manhandling of Ben. "Hey, hands off my merchandise, missy," she called out.

I let Ben go and pointed a finger at him. "There will be payback. You won't know when. You won't know where. But it's comin'."

He lifted his left eyebrow. "You're trying to start a prank war with me? The king of pranks?"

The man had a point. He knew how to play it cool and had the patience of a sphinx. No one suspected him or respected his devious mind. He possessed a talent for passing off the blame for pranks onto others and excelled at the long con. We found out after graduation that *he* had been the instigator of the pimple hex in high school, not young Gerald Tanner. Ben was the provider of the face cream to cure the unsightly acne, so we thought he was our savior, not the sinner. He not only fooled us all but he also made a lot of money off his efforts. Had he not told us himself, we may never have known.

"Maybe not," I acquiesced.

"Still, I'm sorry she made you drink that stuff. But consider that it might have helped you, whether there's something wrong with you or not. That's a win-win in my book." Ever the advocate, Ben talked his way out of trouble.

I bid my friends goodbye and went on a search for Dash. Waving through the cafe window at the people surrounding Flint, I wondered where Juniper and Horatio had ended up tonight. Had I been able to catch them after the debates, I would have invited them to come with us. I hoped they knew they still had many friends supporting them in Honeysuckle.

I spotted a motorcycle parked in front of the bar and crossed the street in that direction, my blood quickening at the thought of getting to ride behind Dash again. As I got closer, I detected two bikes instead of one. And neither of them was like the one I'd ridden on today.

The shattering of glass from the alley between the bar and the next building stopped me from entering The Rainbow's End. I followed the noise of angry voices and witnessed a struggle at the end of the passageway. Ducking behind the dumpster, I stood up to see over the bags of trash.

Two dark figures took on one, fists hitting flesh in muted thuds. The one getting beaten bent over with a blow to his stomach, groaning.

"Stay out of our business," warned one of the attackers.

"You can't tell me what to do anymore," grunted the other attacker, pounding his knuckles across the one in the middle's face with a crack.

A roar ripped out of the punching bag. Amber eyes I recognized flashed in the darkened alley. *Dash*. With a snarl, the wolf shifter straightened to his full height and tossed the first guy in my direction. A hard body hit the other side of the dumpster with a crash, pushing the metal container into me. I flinched and crouched down.

Taking the guy who had punched him in the face by the throat, Dash threw him up against the brick wall with a growl. His voice hovered between human and animal, and he rasped, "Tell me why you're in my town, Trey, or I will break you."

The man who had taken a glorious motorcycle ride with me earlier today no longer existed. Based on the grunts and heavy panting, his animal fought against him to break free. And was winning.

Pixie Poop.

Chapter Seventeen

Unsure of what to do, I slipped my phone from my pocket and flipped it open, steadying my thumb over the middle Menu button and giving thanks for Lee's genius brain over and over in my head.

The one Dash called Trey struggled to be set free and gasped out his words. "Let...me go." With a twist and a grunt, he planted his foot against Dash's torso and kicked, breaking free. He held up his hands to stop another attack. "Give me a chance to answer."

The dark figure on the other side of the dumpster rose with a rolling growl. He shook himself off and cursed at Dash, promising to end his life. I looked around me for anything I could use to beat him with. A stick or broken bottle at least. Unfortunately, Lucky was too fussy of a leprechaun to allow much mess around his bar. My magic would have to be enough, but the second I used it on either one of the guys, I would become a target for the other.

"Cool it, Butch, and keep your wolf in check," Trey demanded. "No point in making a scene. Let me talk to Dash first. Go back inside and finish your beer."

The hulking shadow in front of me curled his hands into fists. "He has no right to give us orders. He ain't our alpha. We ain't got one anymore, remember?"

So they were both shifters like Dash? A smart girl would avoid trouble and run from the scene to get help. But I wanted to know more. Needed to hear what this Trey had to say and why Dash knew him. I kept my spell phone at the ready just in case but stayed hidden to listen.

Trey's eyes flashed a color similar to Dash's. "Maybe not now. But he used to be mine, and I owe him. I'll be fine."

"I can't leave you here alone with him," complained Butch.

Dash lifted the corner of his lips with another snarl. "What if I promise not to harm a hair on his pretty head until he's done talkin'? Alpha's honor."

Trey waved his friend off. "Beat it, Butch. I'll come get you when I'm done."

The big guy turned in my direction to leave, and my stomach dropped. I suppressed the scream of alarm building in my throat as hard as I could.

"Not that way, you idiot." Trey pointed to the side door. "Go to the bathroom and wipe off any blood first. We don't need anyone else gettin' any ideas."

Butch stomped off away from me, complaining under his breath and shooting another warning that he'd be coming back out to kick Dash's behind if Trey wasn't inside in the next fifteen minutes, whole and pristine. The side door to the bar closed shut with a clang, and the two men left in the alley faced off.

Trey scoffed. "You might wanna be careful about sayin' anything about being an alpha or having an ounce of honor to promise. You're the one that left us behind, deserter."

Dash rushed at him, knocking him back into the brick wall and pinning him with his arm that looked far too furry. "Call me that again, and I will end you." Light glistened off the string of saliva that dripped from his elongating fangs.

"The truth hurts, doesn't it," Trey managed, staying calm in contrast to Dash, fighting to keep his animal at bay.

"I did what I had to," protested Dash.

In frustration, Trey broke free and got in Dash's face. "Which was what? To take a functioning pack and gut it? Do you know what happened after you left us? Do you know who sits as alpha of the Red Ridge pack right now?" He stepped close enough that his nose almost touched Dash's. "Do you even want to know? Or are you having too good of a time hiding away in this tiny town to care?"

Dash growled and pushed Trey away, but his head hung low. Panting, he gritted his teeth. "Tell me."

"Only out of the debt from when you saved my life all those years ago when we were young pups, and not because the man that stands in front of me has earned crap." Trey crossed his arms. "It's your brother running the pack now."

Dash huffed. "I know. I made sure to leave Davis in charge before I left. So what's the problem? My youngest brother should be running a clean pack."

Trey's wry grin highlighted by the streetlamp from the end of the alley sent shivers down my back. "Wrong brother."

A string of curses flew into the night air, and Dash screamed long and loud until he ran out of breath, ending in a pained howl.

Trey continued without giving Dash a break. "Cash turned the entire pack into his personal ATM. He forces all of the members to make money any way they can. Turns out, he has a real head for business." Trey spat on the ground.

"Of the darker variety, I'd bet." Dash swore again. "He always had a thing for booze, drugs, and unsavory women."

"Hey, when everyone longs for the days when your father was alpha, you know they all feel the hot flames from down below lickin' at their furry butts." Trey ran his hand through his hair. "Look, man. I get why you left. Survival and all that. And you'd been through enough, tryin' to fix the pack after what happened to your mom."

My mind raced, attempting to swim against the flood of information. The little I knew about pack politics came from Dash, and I knew he had no love for his family except the unconditional devotion to his mother. The darkness he'd warned me about time and again—maybe I should have listened. The man I'd wrapped my arms around on the motorcycle with unabashed trust rode off into the distance, far away from the one with the haunted shadow on his face, standing in front of me.

"So why are you here in Honeysuckle? Is the pack makin' moves out this far?" Dash asked.

Trey sighed. "No. I went rogue, like you. Had to find a way to make my own money to keep my family safe, and maybe give them a chance to leave, too. Dina's in her second year at Red Ridge State, and I'll do anything to keep her future clean."

"Your little sister's old enough to be in college?"

Trey's shoulder's relaxed. "Can you believe it?"

"I'll bet she's a looker," ventured Dash, earning him a light punch against his arm. Their shared past brought a temporary peace between the two shifters.

"Better than me, if you can believe such beauty exists," chuckled Trey. He took a deep breath and blew it out. "Look, if my being here is a problem for you, Butch and I will leave. He'll give me a bunch of grief, but it's nothin' I can't handle."

After a long pause, Dash nodded. "I'd appreciate it."

Trey clapped him on the shoulder. "You know, you still hit like a female pup," he joked.

"I dominated you the whole time," bantered Dash. "Just like the old days." He walked forward and opened the side door to the bar.

I couldn't make out the underlying emotion underneath the glance Trey shot him from behind, but the hairs on the back of my arms stood on end. "Yeah. Like the old days."

Dash held the door open for him. "I'll be with you in a sec. Have to check on somethin' first." His head swiveled in my direction.

Pixie poop. I ducked back down, hiding behind the edge of the dumpster. Listening for the metal side door to shut, I held my breath. It clanked into place, and I thanked my luck, standing up to leave.

"You have a serious problem." Dash's muscled frame took up all the air around me.

"You're bleeding," I replied, unable to come up with a different response. I reached out to wipe the blood from the corner of his lip, and he flinched away. My heart sank with the sudden move.

"I'll heal. What were you thinkin' hanging around three fighting shifters, Charli?"

"I...I heard the commotion, and then I thought I could help you," I offered.

He snorted. "Exactly how? By shooting one of your sparking hexes at them? You could have done more harm than good."

"I could have done something," I complained.

"But you didn't. You sat there, watching and listening. Hearing things that should never have followed me here." He cast his eyes down with a frown and shook his head. "It's done now."

I swallowed hard, not knowing what he was declaring over. I wanted to understand the stories behind Trey's words, to get to know Dash's history. Even if it meant I had to be exposed to darkness, maybe I could offer him some light.

"Go home, Charli." Dash refused to look at me.

"Not until I know you're okay." I touched his arm. "*Talk* to me, Dash. Let me help."

A smile spread across his lips, but it held no joy. His eyes flashed, and his teeth sharpened into fangs, his nose appearing to grow a bit longer. A low noise rumbled in his chest, vibrating so hard that it shook through me. The animal in him threatened me with a growl, and I jumped. With a little effort, he hid his other half again.

"Finally. The right response to me. I know that you think Honeysuckle is a safe place as you skip to your grandmother's house on a regular basis. But, dammit, you're not Little Red Riding Hood, and this ain't a fairy tale." He glared at me like a predator, his eyes burning in the dark. "When are you gonna get that I am the big bad wolf, and eventually, I will hurt you. Go. Home."

Quick anger boiled my blood and adrenaline rushed through me. I burst forward and grabbed his arm, yanking as hard as I could to turn him to face me. "Fine. You don't want me by your side, then let me ask you a couple of important questions. What are you doing fighting with them in the first place? Is this a shifter territory thing? And why are you just letting them go? I don't think you pressed hard enough about why they were here in the first place."

Dash looked down at my hand grasping his bicep. He flexed once, making the muscle too big to hold on to, and my grip slipped. "First, I don't have a territory. Nothing here that I care enough to protect from others."

His words stung, and I rubbed the spot over my heart. I thought I caught him wince as he watched me.

"Second," he continued, "I've known Trey most of my life. If there were something wrong, he would have told me there at the end. He's promised to go, and that's good enough. So, go home, Charli."

"No." I stomped my foot.

His eyebrow quirked up. "Did you just stomp your foot at me? Like a small child?"

I stared him down. "I was expressing my unwillingness to be told what to do."

"Like a bratty little girl." He sneered. "You are a head case. They should lock you up, not crazy old women. Whenever someone yells fire, you run straight into the flames. You have to stop putting yourself in the path of danger. And tonight, any number of times you could have gotten hurt. For the last time, go home, Charli."

"Stop telling me what to do. You're not *my* alpha." Hearing the words I uttered, I covered my mouth, horrified at the ammunition I'd launched at him. "Oh, Dash. I didn't mean that."

He took a step away from me into a patch of darkness, hiding again. "No matter what you heard, you still know nothing," he gritted.

"Because you won't tell me. No one keeps a secret as well and as long as you do. You give me glimpses in the sun only to dive into the shadows the second you open up." I stepped forward, unwilling to give up on the hurting man. "Stop running. Explain to me what you think I heard, in your own words. Help me understand. Let me be here, supporting you."

Tension crackled between us. I left the choice up to him, either to let me ride with him as his partner or to leave me behind. When the silence stretched, I closed my eyes and repeated my desires to myself.

Soft lips kissed the top of my head, and with a curse under his breath, Dash wrapped his strong arms around me. I breathed in his scent of sweat, blood, and *him*. His beard tickled the back of my neck as he squeezed me tighter.

Too soon, he let me go, and I bit my lip, readying myself to break through his barriers once and for all. To be let in to see all of him—the good and the bad. When I searched his eyes for acceptance, all hope drained out of me.

His hands dropped to his side, curling in and out of fists. "I'm no good for you, Charli." His stern countenance softened for a second with sadness.

With caution, I lifted my hand to his face and caressed his cheek. "Why don't you let me make that decision?" My voice came out so soft that I couldn't be sure he heard me.

He closed his eyes, and for a brief moment, he nuzzled into my touch. "Because I'm the fire that burns down everything that matters and turns it into ashes." With an aching sigh, he placed his hand over mine and removed it. "Go home, Charli."

I backed off with quick feet so he wouldn't notice the

tears pooling in my eyes. Turning, I walked away, knowing he watched every step I took. Counting on his superior shifter hearing, I stopped and shot one last bullet at him. "Dash, you know when you told me you would hurt me?"

"Yeah," he replied.

"You just did."

Chapter Eighteen

I woke up in my bed, covered in my favorite quilt. The last thing I remembered was rocking on the porch alone. At some point, I must have fallen asleep, and someone had carried me upstairs. For now, I wallowed in my bad mood, replaying my failures like a broken record. Unable to face the bright new morning, I pulled the quilt over my head, wondering who had changed me out of my clothes and into a long T-shirt.

A light knock on my bedroom door interrupted my dedicated boohoo bash. "Birdy. You still in bed? Get up. TJ has already made you breakfast and is out mucking stalls while your lazy bones sleep." Matt waited for a response. When he didn't get one, he rapped his knuckle on the wood a little harder. "Come on, Charli."

"Go away," I managed with a voice as dry as a desert.

Smacking my lips, I marveled at my dragon breath and how parched I was. Probably due to the dehydration from expelling all the water inside of me through my eyes last night.

My brother switched to rapid pounding, beating an annoying rhythm. "I can do this all day," he threatened.

Throwing off my quilt, I pulled on a pair of shorts and switched out of the oversized shirt into a simple tank top. I yanked the door open and caught Matt off guard, about to knock again. "You stink like a pound of unicorn manure." I narrowed my one open eye at him.

He sniffed his shirt in jest. "I don't think so. No unicorns out in the barn yet. Only horses, and TJ still won't let me help her. Nice hair, by the way." He reached out and messed it up even more. "Fix yourself up into somethin' presentable and come downstairs, please. We need to talk."

I ran a brush through my hair and squirted toothpaste in my mouth, swishing it around to get rid of the stench, not caring enough to do more. When I finished in the bathroom, I plodded my way to the kitchen. My stomach rumbled at the feast waiting for me. If I couldn't ignore the day and spend it under my quilt, I could eat my depression away. With messy scoops, I filled my plate.

Matt poured both of us a cup of coffee, even taking the time to fix mine exactly how I liked it with a little sugar and milk. He sat across from me, sipping his on his drink and saying nothing. I ignored him, digging into the cheesy grits with crumbled bacon on top, mixing in a bite of scrambled eggs. My stomach remembered it was hungry, and I couldn't get enough to eat, scarfing down all the savory contents of my plate.

The back door opened, and Beau walked in. "Oh, excuse me. At this late hour, I didn't expect to find anyone in here."

"Where've you been? Don't tell me you were at the retirement home." I regarded his guilty face. "You know you're not supposed to go there."

My roommate joined us at the table, picking up a piece of bacon. He sniffed it first before eating it in two crunches. "Mm. I know we vampires don't have to eat regular food, but there is something magical about the parts of a pig."

"Don't change the subject. Where did you go last night?" Matt pressed.

Beau glanced between my brother and me. "I visited the Widow Macintosh at her house after I got Charli here all tucked up in bed. Don't worry. I haven't been back to the home."

Matt switched his gaze to me. "Why did he have to help you up to bed?"

"I think the bigger question is how in the world you can romance so many women, Beau," I deflected, changing the focus.

"I told you before, I understand loneliness. Not everything is about passion. It's about knowing how to pay someone attention, making them feel important because they are."

"So you don't do that vampire hypnotizing thing I've heard about?" Matt joked.

Beau stood up in a huff. "I see I'm going to have to educate you in the same manner as your sister. Let me put it in a way the two of you can better understand. Do you consider yourselves brother and sister?"

"Of course," I answered.

Matt spoke up at the same time, "Yes."

"And yet, you don't share the same blood. You don't have the same magical abilities, and I'm sure you have different strengths. It's much the same with vampires. We are different beings with differing lives. Our abilities can be similar, but they can also be vastly distinct from one another." He poofed into a bat and back again. "I can transform myself like that, but others cannot. Some can function at a higher acceleration than others, making them look like they have super speed, appearing here and there without being noticed.

"I get it. I need to stop generalizing," I said.

Beau cut me off. "I'm not finished. The ability you're talking about, holding another being in a vampire's thrall, is not seen as an acceptable talent to use. It is extremely difficult for both the vampire and the subject. The vampire must stay close by to control whomever they have enthralled. And those poor souls...well, their stories don't tend to end well. Add all of those factors up, and you piece together a problem for our kind. The threat of being discovered, hated, and hunted again."

Matt processed the information. "I may never look at Raif the same again."

"Oh, you don't have to worry about him. It's not something he can do, plus, he's too concerned about what others think to ruin his reputation." My roommate stole another piece of bacon, his lesson finished.

"So he wouldn't try anything like that on the whole town, just to win the election, right?" I asked.

Beau swallowed and shook his head. "No way. Raif may be...well, him. But he follows the rules to a fault. Okay, you two, I'm off to get some beauty sleep. Sorry I interrupted your meal."

I'd get on him later about his help in getting me to bed, and then give him explicit instructions to leave me in my clothes next time. The kitchen quieted down, and I got back to eating, deep in thought.

My brother quietly drank his coffee, his breath the only thing I could hear besides the birds twittering in the magnolia tree outside. He didn't utter a word when I snagged the last cinnamon roll off a plate in the middle of the table or dumped the rest of the bacon onto my plate. Annoyed, I chucked a strip at him, and it bounced off his forehead.

"What's wrong with you?" I cried.

"I'm waiting."

"For what?"

He picked up the bacon and shoved it in his mouth. "For you to tell me what's been up your behind these past few days."

My defenses snapped to attention and my anxiety from everything that had happened—or not happened—in the past few days kicked in. Picking up my plate, I placed it in the sink with a clatter. "Tell TJ thanks for breakfast." I hustled out of the kitchen, afraid of what might come next.

"Birdy," he yelled after me. "Frosted fairy wings, Charli, stop!"

My foot hovered over the first step, my body coiled to sprint back upstairs. As much as I wanted to run and hide, I couldn't. Not from Matt. We'd been through too much together for me not to recognize the hurt in his voice.

He took my hand from the banister and held it in his. "Remember how Mom used to always know right when we needed a hug? Or how Dad produced ice cream out of nowhere to cheer us up? Now that I'm older, I know that it wasn't because they had some sort of special magic or a crystal ball. It's not hard to see when the ones you love are hurting. Talk to me, Birdy."

An empty sob burst out of me, but no tears came. Matt squeezed my hand three times, our family's silent way of saying *I love you*, and pulled me into a quick hug. "Come on."

Leading me out onto the porch, he directed me to sit in a rocking chair and took the one beside me. The rhythmic creak of the chairs swaying calmed me down. My brother's presence reminded me of the strength our family possessed.

"When you came home the other night," Matt started, "you looked like you wanted to tell me something. And then I went and ruined it by complaining about my own issues."

"You have a right to tell me you're anxious. You're going to be called Dad soon by your own little girl. Better start stocking up on the ice cream now." I smiled for the first time this morning. Lifting my legs and hugging my knees into me, I folded in on myself in the chair. "Ah, Matty D. I think I'm broken."

My brother didn't try to change my mind or tell me I was wrong. He waited for me to continue on my own, staring out onto the land in front of us, still rocking.

All my worries about my magic and my fears of not having them anymore spilled out of me. I told him every detail, leaving out what had happened with Dash last night. One, I didn't want my brother to have to act in a warden capacity with the shifter. And two, I couldn't guarantee that Matt wouldn't find him to hex his behind. Or kick it. Or both.

"You know, Ms. Alma isn't the only person to file a stolen item report with us at the station. There are at least six more complaints, and they aren't all jewelry either. Come to think of it, Mimsy Blackwood pulled me aside after the debates and told me that she was worried because she couldn't find her antique set of teaspoons in her buffet," he observed.

"That can't be a coincidence, can it? I mean, six reports or maybe more, all filed at the same time." I let go of my legs and gripped the arms of the chair. "Matt, could someone be breaking into people's houses and stealing from them?"

"As a warden, I'm trained not to rule out any possibility. But for each of these cases, there's absolutely no sign of a break in."

"If my talents weren't broken, then maybe I could have helped instead of failing," I lamented.

"Stop saying you failed. And you're not broken. Maybe your ego is a little bruised, but I know you better than anybody. I've never known you to lie down and give up or hide under your quilt for long. And you know what Dad always said," my brother needled me.

"You only fail if you stop tryin'." The old mantra rung in my ears. "You gonna tell your daughter that?"

"If I can be half the father to her that Dad was for us, then I will be lucky." Matt knocked on the wood of his rocker for good measure.

"I've been meanin' to ask, have you been by Nana's recently?" I checked.

"Yesterday. But she was running out the door, so I didn't really get to talk to her. The election and everything that's happened since it started is beginning to take its toll on her."

Matt didn't have to tell me he was worried about our grandmother. I was, too, but saying that out loud to each other might mean that something was really wrong with her, and we couldn't handle that.

"The election," I mused. "First Mrs. K's outburst. Then her death. Finding her body in the library, which made Horatio look guilty as implied by Linsey in the *Honeysuckle Holler*. Add to that, people seem to be missing stuff that's valuable to them."

"And to others. Some of the items could fetch a high price outside of our town," my brother added.

"Oh," I exclaimed. "Mrs. K's brooch. It's missing, too. Mason wanted me to try finding it, but...you know."

Matt regarded me. "You were scared you might fail again."

In front of Mason, I added internally. I nodded at my brother. "I think it's important that the piece of jewelry is found."

"You think the missing goods and Mrs. K's death might be connected?" Matt looked off into the distance deep in thought. "It's not a bad theory, but none of the people who have filed a report have anything to do with the election. And our former teacher's death seems all about it. I don't know if there's enough evidence to support that speculation."

I held up my finger. "Yet. Give me a sec." Jumping off the chair, I bounded upstairs and searched the pocket of the pants I was wearing the night before. Grabbing my desired item, I ran back to join my brother.

"What's that?" he stared at the device in my hand.

"It's a spell phone. Lee came up with the idea."

"I want one." He reached out to take mine, and I slapped his hand away. Flipping the phone open, I selected the relevant name and pressed the green icon button.

"Charli," Mason said on the end of the line. "What can I do for you?"

"Do you still have Mrs. Kettlefields' stuff in your office?" I asked.

"No." He sounded interested. "But I can put my hands on it in mere minutes. Why?"

I glanced at Matt who flashed a smile that definitely

reminded me of Dad. "Because I'm going to find out where the brooch is."

"When can you get here?" The detective's voice snapped into business mode.

"I'll hop on my bike as soon as we hang up."

"Good," Mason replied, ending the call.

Matt high-fived me and snatched the device from my other hand. "You want me to take you to the station instead?" he offered, already messing with the spell phone.

"No. I've got this." My churning gut didn't agree with me one hundred percent, but I had to try.

"If you need me, I'll be there for you. But I'm pretty sure you won't. You can do this, Birdy." He tossed the phone back to me. "Tell Lee I'm next in line to get one of those."

◊

MASON CROSSED THE ROOM, dragging the box of Mrs. K's items across his desk in my direction. "No time like the present. Choose something and test things out. If your magic works, then you'll know it was a temporary glitch. Something you can examine later."

"If it doesn't?" I put my fear right out in front of both of us.

He squeezed my hand, holding it for a second longer than normal. "If it doesn't, then I'll help you figure it out. Either way, I'm right here with you."

Doubt crept back in through the cracks in my emotional

armor. What if I failed, and the man with the warm hand wrapped around mine stopped believing in me?

Mason let me go. "Let's not give you a chance to back out." He popped the top off the box and took out items, placing them one by one in front of me. Her cloying scent still clung to each one.

"Not the perfume." I squeezed my nose shut with my fingers. "It took way too long to wash it off last time it got on my skin. No, I need to find something that's personal to her. Something she valued."

The detective opened up a drawer in his desk. "What about her diary?" He took out the journal disguised as the *History of Magic* textbook and handed it to me.

It felt a little like a violation of my former teacher's emotions, using her words to anchor my efforts. But it couldn't get more personal than her own scribbled thoughts other than holding her hand, and we were *not* going there.

I picked up the book, my fingers rubbing the worn cover. At least the food from breakfast provided me with lots of fuel. Breathing in deep, I centered myself, composing a careful rhyme in my head, needing as much help as I could possibly get.

"Heed my words and listen well, as I weave my magic spell. Against myself, I will not rail. For this one task, I cannot fail. To find the brooch, I need to see. Oh, magic gift, please work for me."

Gathering my energy inside, I willed my powers to life. Gripping the diary in my hands until the pressure hurt, I shut my eyes closed and gave my magic a chance to work.

With a gasp, I dropped the book. It fell to the floor with a thunderous thud.

"What happened? It didn't work?" Mason asked, reaching out to me.

"The exact opposite," I said. "I know exactly where to go."

Chapter Nineteen

Mason decided against alerting the other wardens. He alone accompanied me, sensing the importance of the task. I didn't have to follow the path of a glowing thread to find the missing piece. Images had revealed themselves to me with strong clarity, connecting me to the location without me having moved a muscle. We arrived at the house together, and I sat in the car, staring at the white picket fence with pink flowers gushing over it, wishing my magic hadn't worked at all. The detective knocked on the door.

Flint answered, his face brightening. "Charli. Detective Clairmont. What are you doing here?" When he caught sight of our faces, he stopped smiling. "Is there something wrong?"

"Mr. Hollyspring, I need to enter your premises with Ms. Goodwin." Mason's cold professionalism kicked in.

"You're always welcome. Please." He opened his door wider and ushered us inside. "Goss, honey, we have visitors," he called out.

I protested her presence. With her pregnancy, she didn't need the worry. At the same time, if I found the brooch where I thought—no, *knew*—it was, she'd have enough to upset her.

"Please stand back and allow Ms. Goodwin to work," Mason insisted.

"What's going on?" Goss joined us in their living room. Before she could utter another word, Flint reached out to hold her hand, enduring a nervous sprinkling of pink dust.

"Charli, please." Mason held out his hand, insisting that I do what I came here to do.

Drawing on a sliver of my magic, I captured the clear, glowing thread that formed. It tugged on me without much effort, and I followed its beckoning into the kitchen and straight to the counter. A ceramic unicorn head sat on the surface, and I pulled it to me, grasping it by its horn and opening the vessel. The scent of cinnamon filled my nose as I emptied the container of every last Snickerdoodle. At the very bottom of the cookie jar lay the brooch.

"Don't touch it," warned Mason, joining me at my elbow.

He spellcast a protective shield around the piece of jewelry and dumped it out. It clattered on the counter, its metal and simple jewels sparkling.

"What is that?" asked Goss.

Ignoring the slight shake of the detective's head, I

answered, "It's Mrs. K's brooch she received when she retired."

Flint stroked his beard, his brow furrowed. "What's it doing there?"

Mason pursed his lips. "Mr. and Mrs. Hollyspring, I need to take you to the warden station with me. If you come voluntarily, there doesn't need to be any drama. But I have to take you in."

The gnome stepped in front of his wife. "Take me. She has nothing to do with it."

"And you do?" Mason asked.

Flint opened his mouth to answer but closed it without a ready explanation. He hung his head. "She's having terrible morning sickness. Can't you just take me?"

"Or how about you hold on a second while we think things through," I suggested, raising an eyebrow at the detective. "None of this makes any sense."

"I can't ignore my responsibilities. Neither is under arrest yet, but they have to be brought in. I thought you understood this, Charli." He regarded the distraught couple for a beat, his frosty distance thawing a bit. "Listen, I'm willing to take you in, Flint, and leave your wife here in your home to keep her from being under too much duress. Mrs. Hollyspring, please do not go anywhere for the time being." The detective waited for the gnome.

Flint consoled his wife and promised that everything would be okay. In that touching moment, they broke my heart, and I hated that my magic had done this to them.

In desperation, I pulled Mason into the living room. "You can't do this."

"I thought you wanted Mrs. K's death solved. Well, you helped find a crucial piece to the puzzle. Congratulations. But this is my job, Charli." He frowned in disappointment.

"I know. But it's too convenient. First, Horatio looks guilty. Now, Flint will if word gets out. Both are involved in the election. The puzzle pieces fit too well." My words flew out of my mouth to try and keep up with my brain.

"What about Occam's razor?" he asked.

I remembered Horatio's explanation. "The simplest answer is usually the right one, I know. But what if it's *too* simple? This is more like someone just handed you not only the answers to the test but also all of the questions, too. And what about my part in all this?"

Mason sighed. "I know you don't like the results because it affects your friends, but aren't you relieved that your magic worked?"

"But that's the thing. It didn't before. And now all of a sudden, bam, it worked better than ever. Right when it needed to." A sudden thought caught me off guard, and I tugged on Mason's shirt. "What if I had tried to use my magic that time before in your office?"

"Then you would have found the brooch just the same."

I turned my finger in the air, trying to get him to follow the logic to the next step. "And then Flint's participation in the election would be—"

"In jeopardy," he completed. "Taking him out of the running."

"Like Horatio," I added. "This has all been about the election. It has to be. And there are only two more candidates left, one being a very likely guilty party."

"Now you're moving from theory to biased accusation. I know you don't hold any affection for Raif, but your dislike of him isn't foolproof evidence."

I kept the fact that I wasn't thinking of the vampire to myself. My theories and efforts had already gotten my friends in trouble. I needed to investigate on my own before I threw another one under the bus.

Mason continued. "I do see where you're going with this, and I will consider the possibilities. But for now, I have to follow the evidence I have in hand." He held up the brooch. "Mr. Hollyspring, if you please."

Goss exploded into hot tears and pink fairy dust in protest. I went to her side, holding onto her hand to watch her husband leave. When we all got to the door, an unexpected visitor waited for us.

"Detective Clairmont, is it true that you've nabbed the murderer of Mrs. Kettlefields? And Flint, why did you feel the need to get rid of her?" Linsey hounded them, following close on their heels as Mason escorted Flint to his vehicle.

I slammed the door shut and pulled the fairy deeper into the interior of her house. "Goss, whatever you do, do *not* answer the door until whoever it is identifies themselves. Even then, you may want to wait until Flint is home."

"You're gonna stay with me, right?" Her little wings quivered.

"I'm going to go find Ben and get him down to the station." Guilt gnawed on me. If I had to pay out of my own pocket, I would make sure that Flint had an advocate on his side. "Pixie poop," I exclaimed. "Mason was my ride."

Goss sniffed and pulled herself together. "If it's to help my Flinty, then here." With a flourish of her hand, her wand appeared. She waved it a couple of times and opened a door onto the fairy path.

I stepped through to a spot on Main Street, looking back to see her floating on the other side. "Thank you," she managed before bursting into tears. The sparkling pink magical portal dwindled and closed.

With little time to lose, I rushed past everyone and made it to Jed and Ben's office, panting. After enlisting my friend's help, I left, unsure of what to do next. The clock on the front of the town hall chimed. Lunchtime, although my appetite no longer existed.

I spotted Dash's motorcycle parked in front of The Rainbow's End. The other two I'd seen before were gone. Fixing things with the shifter needed to be the next thing on my list. Maybe I could bribe him to talk to me with some food at the cafe.

I entered Lucky's bar and found the leprechaun out of sorts. He snorted. "Good, yer here. Take your furry friend and get him outta my place."

Scanning the bar, I couldn't spot anyone I knew. A door

banged open, and Dash stumbled out of one of the bathrooms in the back. "You know, it's hard to hit a bulls-eye when the target's movin'," he slurred.

"How long has he been here?" I asked Lucky.

"Since last night. He never left, even after his shady comrades did. Drank until he passed out cold in his seat, so I let him sleep it off in me office." The leprechaun's Irish accent got thicker in his irritation. "But when I tried to shoo him out this mornin', he threatened to go behind the bar to drink the libations. Broke a bottle or two already. I've been servin' him beer to keep him from drinkin' me outta my business."

"H-e-e-y, Charli's here." The drunken shifter spotted me. "What's a hot place doin' in a girl like you? Wait a minute," he frowned. "That's not right." A belch thundered out of him, and he hiccuped at the end. Pointing a finger at me, he blinked hard to focus. "You're not a girl. You're a woman. A feisty one. I like feisty. Rawr." He made a cat-like sound at me and attempted a wink.

"I thought wolves growled, not purred," I responded, not amused.

His lower lip jutted out. "But I growled at you last night, and you left me."

"You *told* me to leave. Demanded for me to go home. Repeatedly," I yelled.

Dash staggered toward me. "That's right. Had to hurt you to make you go because you keep tryin' to fix me. I can't be fixed. Too damaged." He scrubbed his hand down his face.

"Need to drink more. Want to forget that I hurt my family. That I screwed up the pack. That I can't have you."

He wobbled and swayed where he stood. I feared he might break me if I tried to carry him out. "Lucky, I don't think I can handle him on my own."

"Then call yer brother or one of the other wardens. He can't stay here," insisted the leprechaun.

If Matt had one of Lee's spell phones, this would be much easier to keep quiet. Then again, maybe the spectacled genius could use his intellect to solve the problem of a drunken wolf shifter.

I took out my phone, hit a button, and spoke into it. "Lee, it's Charli. Dash is drunk at Lucky's. Come get him." I sent the text and headed for the door.

"Leavin' me again?" Dash asked. "That's right. You have to. 'Cause I'm no good. No good." He repeated the phrase over and over in a slur.

Unable to take it anymore, I walked up to him and slapped his face as hard as I could. My hand ached from the impact, and I cradled it.

No growl. No flashing amber eyes. Not one hair morphing into fur. He touched his face and rubbed it. "Ow."

"Did it hurt?" I shouted. "Good. Then maybe you'll understand a fraction of how you've made me feel. I have more important things to deal with than your pity party of one. Get your life straightened out, Dash."

I rushed to the door and shoved it open. My hand pounded, but I pushed down the pain. Trying not to draw attention to myself by losing my cool in the middle of town, I drew in deep breaths to refocus.

Whoever was taking things had access to all the places. He or she could slip in and out without being noticed, or perhaps they were invited in to begin with. I knew of one person who had that ability *and* whom I had witnessed doing something odd at my grandmother's house.

Unwilling to waste more time, I stole Lily's bike from in front of Mimsy's Whimsies and headed to Nana's place to confirm my suspicions.

Chapter Twenty

Vaulting off my friend's borrowed bike, I dropped it into the azalea bushes. I bounded up the porch steps and burst into my grandmother's house.

"Nana." My voice bounced off the walls and echoed. "Nana, are you home?" I raced through each of the rooms downstairs, unable to find her.

The scent of something burning led me to the kitchen. A cast iron skillet sat on top of the burner, the charred remains of some chicken no longer frying but scalding and smoking in the hot oil. I turned off the stove, the pit of my stomach dropping. A tall glass of sweet tea sat at the end of the kitchen table, condensation dripping down its sides. Panic surged through my chest, and my rapid heartbeat drummed in my ears.

A small sniffling sound alerted me. Quieting down, I

listened for it again. High-pitched whimpering echoed from the second floor, and I sprinted upstairs. My grandmother lay on the hardwood in the hallway, her body sprawled out in an unnatural position. A tiny figure hovered over her.

"I didn't do it, Charli. I swear." Juniper blubbered. "She was like this when I came in."

Taking out my spell phone, I held the Menu button down hard until my thumb hurt. "Get away from my grandmother," I spit out.

Blue-green dust sprinkled off her shivering wings, covering my Nana's face. "Please, let me explain."

A hundred things I could do to her flooded my head, all of them with the intent to cause harm. But none of them would get the information I needed from her. Okay, maybe some of them would work as a decent torture method.

Unable to tamp down the boiling rage inside, my fingertips sparked. "Oh, you will most definitely talk. But first, I need to know. Is she...is she..." I couldn't finish the question.

Juniper nodded. "She's still alive. Just knocked out. See? She's breathing."

My grandmother's chest rose and fell in rhythmic breaths, and hot tears pooled in my eyes from relief. A sob rose in my throat, but I held it back with a hard swallow.

"Let's say I believe you. That you didn't harm my grandmother. Then what are you doing here?" I asked, my nostrils flaring at my effort to keep from hexing her tiny hiney.

The fairy held up Nana's lucky necklace. "I came to return this."

Rushing forward, I snatched it from her hand. "Why? Because you felt bad after you stole it? That's what you were doing that day when I caught you with it, weren't you?"

Her face dropped. "I would never steal. What you saw wasn't what you think. I wasn't taking the necklace. I had just found it, hidden away."

"Why don't I believe you?" I bellowed, magic flickering off my fingers. The phone I still held in one hand crackled, and a tiny puff of smoke curled out of the device. I dropped it on the floor.

Juniper held up her minuscule hands. "I know this doesn't look good. But you keep seeing only part of the truth."

"And I think that you've been taking things from your clients' homes when you're cleaning," I accused. "You are the only one who has open access to all those places. And you're the only one with a direct connection to the election."

"What?" she squealed. "I have no idea what you're talking about. Why are you saying such things? I thought you were my friend."

My gut twisted in confusion. "I am." But what I'd witnessed with my own eyes couldn't be denied.

"Then you have to trust my word, I would *never* hurt you or your family. And I am not the guilty one. Charli, someone is trying to frame me. You have to believe me," she implored.

The simplest answer was usually right. And finding Juniper here like this made her the obvious culprit for everything. But hadn't I hounded Mason about how things were a little *too* convenient?

Before I said anything else, I bent down to check on Nana. In relief, I watched her sigh and roll on her side with a smile, deep in sleep, as if dreaming of something good.

Satisfied that she wasn't in immediate danger, I gave Juniper a chance. "Why do you think you're being framed?"

The fairy drifted closer to me. "Because I've been noticing things going missing in all of the houses we service, too. I didn't want to accuse my employees without evidence, so I started going behind them when I could, doing my own investigating. Enough was disappearing that I was ready to go to the wardens. That's when I discovered this."

With a gesture of her hand, she produced a wand. A portal appeared with a wave, and on the other side of the opened fairy path, a pile of suspicious items lay in the middle of a closet full of cleaning supplies.

"Is that your place?" I asked.

She nodded with a sniff. "I found it there this morning. Someone is trying to make it look like *I'm* the thief to cover their tracks. But I'm not." She burst into tears, her small body vibrating in the air.

If Mrs. K's brooch was planted, and someone placed those things at Juniper's place of business, then who was doing it and why? Or maybe Juniper was guilty, and she was committing a double bluff by trying to make it look like someone wanted her to get into trouble. Confused, I rubbed my temple.

She held her head in her hands. "What am I going to do, Charli? Wait." Her head popped up, her eyes filling with desperate hope. "Horatio told me that he'd suggested you go into business with your magic. Could I hire you to find out who is behind this?"

"That's not how things work for me," I explained. "And I think it's time that you alert the wardens. If you turn yourself in voluntarily, then you might have a better chance at explaining yourself. If you don't, then you'll put yourself at higher risk."

Hope turned to fear in her alarmed gaze. "I can't. Not until I can prove for sure that it's not me. Otherwise, they'll lock me up." She jerked in circles in the air, searching for a way out.

Wanting to believe my friend, I held up my hands to stop her. "Juniper, look, the wardens are on their way here now. You know that thing I dropped on the floor? It should have alerted them to come here any second. You need to be prepared to go with them."

One final turn and she spotted the shimmering door she'd created still open, offering her an easy exit. Looking back at me, she bit her lip in indecision.

Because of our friendship, I had to try and help. Giving it my best shot, I made my desperate plea. "If you run, the guilt will follow you. Stay and fight for your innocence."

My words hit home, and she backed away from the magical door. Juniper dipped in the air, her head hung in defeat. "Okay."

"Charli, where are you?" Mason's voice cried out. A rush of footsteps pounded on the wooden floor below.

"Stay steady," I cautioned Juniper. "Up here," I directed.

My brother made it to us first. "Nana!" Matt rushed by me and knelt by our grandmother.

Mason stood at my side, his arm extended and power emanating from his hand. "I am arresting you, Juniper, on suspicion of theft and murder."

Juniper squeaked with dread. She struggled against the authority of the wardens' power, more and more dust falling from her desperate efforts. With a squeal bigger than she was, she broke free, blue-green dust exploding off of her.

She circled around and zipped to the portal. Before Mason could do anything, her body disappeared through the opening, and the door began collapsing. Before it vanished, her voice tinkled through the last crack. "I'm sorry. Help me solve this, Charli."

With a light shimmer, the portal evaporated.

Matt lifted Nana from the floor with mindful care and laid her down on her bed. He called Doc Andrews and promised to stay with her.

"Find the fairy," he said to me, venom dripping from his tone.

I nodded. "I will, but I don't think she did this."

"Then figure out who did," my brother demanded. Brushing a strand of hair out of Nana's face, his eyes betrayed his unease. "What if..." His voice cracked, and he couldn't finish his question.

I touched him on his shoulder, squeezing my reassurance. "But she's fine. Stay with her, and I will do everything I can to help. I promise."

Mason waited for me at the bottom of the stairs. "How did she get away?" Frustration rolled off of him.

"I don't know," I chewed on my lip, throwing out an unlikely theory. "Maybe your magic can't hold her because she's much stronger than you think." Something that Lavender had said came back to me. "Hey, maybe we've been underestimating her. What if fairies have greater powers than we imagine? They can rip holes through space. What else can they do?"

"I don't have time to get into a philosophical discussion about what fairies can and can't do. We have to find *one* fairy. Do you know where that portal led to?" Mason pressed.

I held up my finger to give myself a moment to process the newly connecting information. "Lavender said she couldn't detect Juniper's aura. That she has trouble reading fairies in general."

The detective indulged me with restless impatience. "You think that's why she broke free from my warden's power. Fantastic news. And?"

I smacked his arm out of the excitement of realization overtaking me. "And maybe fairies aren't the only ones who have abilities we underestimate."

Mason rubbed his arm where I'd hit him. "I don't follow."

An idea formed, and I rushed out of the house, picking up Lily's bike out of the bushes. "I have to go." If I could prove my guess right, then I could clear my friends' names and catch a murderer all at the same time.

Mason called out to me from the porch. "Wait a minute. You can't leave without telling me where Juniper is. I know she's your friend, but you can't deny that she needs to be questioned. Where is she, Charli?"

I hesitated, pondering whether telling him would be the best choice. Knowing that my fairy friend chose to fly away instead of help herself made up my mind. "Her door to the fairy path opened to her place of business. When you go there and see what there is to find, please remember that I'm pretty sure that she's right. She's being set up to take the fall."

"Zeke," the detective yelled, waiting for the young warden to join him. "Gather a few other wardens and go to Fairy Dust & Clean. See if you can find Juniper there. If not, proceed with caution to Horatio's house. We need to bring the fairy in if she's guilty. And if she's not, then she could be in danger. Go, and let Big Willie know what's going on."

Something about the way he barked out orders impressed me and sent warm tingles I had no time to entertain down to my stomach. "If I figure out what I think I will, I'll let you know immediately on my—" I patted my empty pocket. "Oh, wait, I can't. I fried my spell phone."

"How did you...never mind." He went to his car and opened the passenger door for me. "Hop in. I'm going with you."

"You don't even know where I'm heading." Leaving the bike, I obeyed.

"Wherever it is, I'm sure it's got trouble written all over it. Buckle up," he demanded.

⚜

WE GOT to my house in record time. Calling out for my roommate, I dashed around the rooms with impatience, looking for him.

Beau appeared on the landing upstairs, leaning on the banister. "What?"

I didn't have time to comment on his attire, which consisted of a white undershirt and droopy boxer shorts. A little of his rotund belly peeked out under the slightly too-short shirt. "We need your help."

The vampire scratched his behind, still waking up from his nap. "With what?"

"Just stay there," I directed him, returning to the porch where the detective waited for me. "Mason, do you have anything on you that's personal? Something you have a particular connection with?"

Instead of asking me why, he patted his upper body down. "I don't have anything on me. Wait." He pulled out his wallet and handed me his license. "Here."

I didn't even take it from him. "That's not what I mean. Shoot, I need something of value to test out my magic."

The detective's curious countenance demanded an explanation. I told him what Lavender had said about reading vampires and gave a shortened version of Beau's description about their varying abilities. "I need to run an experiment, and you're going to help me with the control to set the standard," I finished.

Mason caught on. "And then with Beau's help, you can either prove or rule out your theory."

"Exactly."

Holding his wallet, he unfolded the leather and took out something with extra care. He held the object in the palm of his hand, gazing at it with an expression I couldn't read. I reached out to open his fingers so I could see what it was. A simple gold ring lay in the middle. My heart dropped with every sparkle of the diamond in the light.

He watched me with careful eyes. "Charli, there's a long story, and I don't have time to go into it. However you need to use this, please be careful."

I swallowed hard and cleared my throat, attempting to talk without giving away my conflicted emotions. "Uh, actually, you're the one that's going to handle it. Go inside and hide it somewhere in the house. Doesn't matter where."

Staying out on the porch, I paced around. I'd always wanted to see a guy pull out a diamond ring, but it had never occurred to me that when it did happen, it might not be meant for me. I remembered that he'd said before that he had been engaged, but the concept never seemed quite real until now. Why did he carry the ring with him, tucked away in his wallet instead of in his home?

"Finished." Mason approached me with caution. "I, uh, assume you need to hold my hand." He offered me his.

I wiped my own on my pants, getting rid of the nervous sweat. "Yeah." It took more than one deep breath to calm me, and my focus wobbled off center, too caught up in the ring.

"Think of the object you're seeking. Aim all your attention on finding it." Opening one eye, I added, "Try not thinking about where you hid it. The point is for *me* to track it down."

With a last lingering gaze, he nodded and shut his eyes. "Got it."

Too many questions clogged up my brain, killing my ability to cast a rhyming spell. I'd have to rely on my pure talents. In a flash, the ring appeared to me, buried in a box in the bottom of a drawer of a highboy dresser in Tipper's old room. The clear picture in my mind wavered and fizzled when Mason's thumb stroked my skin.

My eyes flew open and caught him observing me. "You almost made me lose it."

"Sorry." Something about his tone suggested he wasn't. "So where is it?"

I called out to Beau and told him where to look. The vampire appeared at the top of the staircase, the ring flashing in his fingers. "Well done. Now what?"

"I want you to take the ring anywhere in the house. For this run, keep it in your hand." I waited a few moments to give my roommate a chance to find a good place to hide. This time when I took Mason's hand, I squeezed it hard. "Same routine, but be good and stay still."

The corner of his mouth twitched. "I'll do my best."

We went through the same motions, and I waited for the detective's ring to appear in my head. Nothing. No line of connection. No sense of the piece of jewelry at all.

"That's what I thought." I let go of Mason, shaking out my hands, my adrenaline pumping through me. "Go tell Beau to leave the ring where it is but to stay in the same room."

When we tried for the third time, I still came up with zero. "Amazing." Finding out the reason why my magic didn't work filled me with relief. I wasn't broken at all. My spirit soared, but we had more to do.

The three of us did a few more tests, moving Beau further and further away from the ring's hiding place. When my roommate stood outside on the porch with us watching me use my talents, I could get a faint sense of the ring's location. "Beau, really? The bathroom?"

"What can I say? I had needs. Did your experiment work?" he asked, heading back inside.

My heart thumped hard in my chest. "Better than I expected. Mason, listen. The number of stolen item reports filed at the same time as the election. My inability to find things like Raif's pug or Ms. Alma's ring. And the sudden return of them to find Mrs. K's brooch. Someone is playing a clever shell game."

"And you think it's a vampire," he said.

"Not just any vampire," I continued. "The one who wants to win more than anything and who conveniently hasn't been affected. And now that you've helped me narrow down how things might have happened, you can see that I'm not accusing out of personal bias."

"You know, you're incredibly inspiring when you get going like that." Mason brushed his thumb against my skin again, reminding me that I still held his hand.

I let him go, my cheeks heating. "I'm a girl of many talents," I dared in the moment.

"And it's a privilege to discover more and more of them, Miss Goodwin." He took a step closer.

Beau returned. "Your ring, Detective." He held out the valuable piece of jewelry, and Mason returned it with care to his wallet. A round worn spot in the leather marked where the ring usually rested. Too many questions, not the right time.

His spell phone rang, and he answered it. "Detective Clairmont. What, Lee? When did he...we're on our way. Yes, I've got Charli with me. Tell everyone to stay clear of him." Ending the call, he grabbed me by the arm and dragged me to his car. "We've got to go. Now."

"Why?"

"Because we have to get to Raif's house." He started his car. "Before a mad troll destroys him and half the town."

Chapter Twenty-One

A roar of indignation thundered from inside Raif's home. Glass and other breakables smashed in loud explosions. A couple of nervous wardens gathered on the front lawn, waiting to come up with a plan to handle the dangerous predicament.

"I should get in there." I pushed through the crowd of magic enforcement.

Mason grabbed my arm. "What are you thinking? There's a raging troll inside, and there's no telling what he'll do."

"It's Horatio. If anyone has the ability to think through a situation, it should be him," I said.

Zeke approached the two of us. "We found Juniper at home with him. When we took her away, he, uh, didn't approve." The young warden flinched as a wooden table smashed through a side window and landed in pieces on the ground outside.

"Somebody has to calm him down. We need to talk to Raif, and that's not gonna happen if Horatio knocks him out...or worse." I didn't want to consider the possibility that my verbose friend might turn savage, but I'd seen what a misfired potion could do to his intellect. No telling how pure rage might affect him.

The rest of my gang, except for Blythe, showed up and broke through the throng of onlookers. They gathered around me, my girls offering me their support while Mason pulled Lee aside for a word.

"I got here as fast as I could from the warden station. What's going on here?" asked Ben.

"An angry troll and a guilty vampire don't mix well," I offered, looking up at my tall friend.

"Oh, good. So potentially more clients," he said with a furrowed brow. "This day keeps getting better."

When he finished, the detective attempted to usher us away from the house.

"You all need to stay back," he insisted.

I ducked under his upheld arm. "Do you have a plan?"

"Not yet."

Another piece of furniture shattered another window and landed on the grass in front of us.

"Then let me try to talk to him. I'll stay in the foyer, far enough out of the danger zone," I promised.

"I doubt that." In frustration, Mason gave in with a sigh.

"Fine. I'm coming with you. The second you could possibly get hurt, it's over. If I tell you to leave, you do it. No questions."

"Sure." I rushed up the steps of the house and entered through the opened door. Approaching with caution, I stuck my head around the corner. "Horatio? Are you here?"

"Yes, he bloody well is," replied Raif, his face twisted with hysteria. "Get him out before he destroys another antique."

Something wooden splintered in the other room. "Tell me why you set my Juniper up and I might spare your furniture. Continue to give false testimony, and I might not spare you," Horatio bellowed.

"I've been trying to tell you it's not me, but you refuse to listen. Do *not* touch that vase," the vampire implored. More shattering.

I crept toward the living room, but Mason held me back. "Do not go in there," he insisted.

"I need Horatio to listen, and my best way to do that is to see him face to face. You've got my back. I trust you." I slinked around the doorway. "Horatio, stop throwing things. I'm coming in."

The noise of destruction ceased, and I spotted the troll holding another item in his hand at the ready. "Charli, you must have deduced by now this scoundrel's guilt. He acts like he is superior to the residents in our humble town, but he robs them behind the scenes." He pointed his finger at Raif. "'*False face must hide what the false heart doth know.*'"

"Quoting Shakespeare does not make you any less of a

monster right now," Raif replied, no longer cringing against the beveled glass hutch.

"You might not want to use words like that right now," I suggested. "Answer his questions, and maybe we can end it right here."

The vampire threw up his hands. "I *have*. I didn't set up the fairy. I don't even know what he's talking about."

Fed up with his game, I fired off my list of accusations. "He's talking about all the valuables disappearing from people's houses. Mrs. K's brooch ending up in Flint's cookie jar. The pile of stolen goods planted at Juniper's place of business. Oh, and a dead body lying in the library. Are you telling me you had nothing to do with any of that? You're the only one who benefits from it all."

"You have reached the exact conclusion I came to, Charli," agreed Horatio.

Raif regarded me with a level of loathing I'd yet to see from him. "You come to my house, daring to speculate? Where is your proof? The death of that poor deluded woman, while tragic, had nothing to do with me."

"You wanted me out of the running, just like you desired to take out Flint and my darling Juniper." Horatio tossed a nearby lamp in the vampire's direction for good measure.

"Watch it," warned Mason from behind me.

"If you think I am so guilty, then why don't you have *her* find all those items? If she thinks it is here in my home, then make her prove it by using her so-called talents," Raif demanded. "Otherwise, all of you need to exit my domicile. Now!" he demanded with sharp authority.

Pixie poop. The vampire had called my bluff. If he did have the stolen goods in his house, I wouldn't be able to find them with my magic.

Mason patted my behind, catching me off guard. "He's got you, but you need to focus on keeping Horatio calm and getting him out of the house."

Ignoring my surprise at the strange contact from the detective, I called out to my enormous friend. "Cooler heads need to prevail here, Horatio."

"But we are far from finished. The inimitable Sherlock Holmes was not wrong. *'Eliminate all other factors, and the one which remains must be the truth.'* He has to be the one behind it all," he insisted.

Raif sneered. "Neither one of you is Holmes nor Watson."

I narrowed my eyes. "And you're not out of the clear yet. Horatio, let's go outside and discuss this further. Leave Raif to the wardens and his sweet precious pug." Looking around, I didn't spot his beloved pet. "Where is Barklay?"

"It's *Sir* Barklay." A trickle of pink sweat dribbled down Raif's temple. "The big oaf must have scared him away."

"And you didn't run after him in a panic?" From what I'd seen after the candidate speeches, the vampire should be inconsolable from losing his dog.

He swallowed hard, his eyes darting about him. "Er, I had other problems to deal with."

An enraged troll definitely counted as a problem. But I

still questioned that Raif wouldn't gather up his pug to protect him. "Where's your dog?"

At the mention of his pet, the vampire's indignant mask slipped a little. His lower lip quivered. "He's gone."

"I don't believe that he ran away without you chasing him. He's the most precious thing to you, and you let him go?" I pushed.

Raif contemplated his choices, glancing around at each of us and realizing his options were dwindling. "You don't understand. He's gone. Taken."

Mason pushed past me. "Who took him?"

The vampire slumped into a nearby chair, holding his head in his hands. "Damien," Raif groaned. "He's the one you're looking for."

"Isn't he your friend?" I asked.

He sat up in his chair, sniffing. "Damien Mallory is *no* friend of mine. It was not my choice for him to be here. Some demon from below must have it out for me. Never in my wildest dreams did I imagine Damien would find me in this small town. Of all the places in the world, I never knew why he chose to come to Honeysuckle, but he did. As soon as he laid eyes on me, I understood that my life as I knew it would be over."

With no more items crashing, the wardens from outside filed in through the door, taking watchful places around us and on the other side of the room. Mason held up his hand to hold them in place. "Why didn't you come to the station and give a report if you suspected him? By staying silent, you've been complicit in whatever he's done."

Raif leaned forward in his chair. "At first, he passed off his presence as wanting to find a new place to live. Knowing his affinity for a more luxurious lifestyle, I didn't believe him. However, he convinced me of his usefulness if I let him stay with me to explore the town more."

"You mean, you thought he could help you win the election," I clarified.

"Yes," he nodded. "I confess, his ability to, shall we say, manipulate the situation at hand did entice me not to protest. He possesses a shrewd mind and knows how to win people over. With Lady Eveline visiting her family in Europe, I needed someone on my side. Damien's skills at helping me shape my campaign made me a front-runner if not the clear choice. After all, we wouldn't be having an election without my insistence in the first place."

Mason started talking, but I interrupted him. "When did you begin to suspect him? There's so much more than an election at stake. A life was taken." My stomach churned, wondering if the vampire had remained quiet in order to stay ahead.

"Let me do the questioning," the detective murmured to me. "But answer her," he directed at Raif.

"I would never have kept quiet had I been sure he was behind Mrs. Kettlefield's demise. I thought the unfortunate woman had done herself harm," the vampire said.

"Despite you benefiting from what the *Honeysuckle Holler* did in implicating me," added Horatio.

"Yes. I figured if foul play was at hand that our team of capable wardens could solve the issue." Raif took a petty shot at Mason and the others in the room. For someone running for office, he didn't have a clue how to win fans. Perhaps Damien had been beneficial to his campaign in toning down the obnoxious side Raif couldn't quite contain.

Mason tensed beside me. "You didn't answer the question. When did you suspect Damien?"

"I heard rumors and concern that someone was breaking into houses when I was talking to the people. They wanted to know what I would do about the town's safety. And my knowledge of Damien's past suggested he might be involved," Raif continued. "But when I finally confronted him about it, he turned on me. Threatened to end my chances in the election and my ability to stay in Honeysuckle if I didn't keep quiet. When it got to be too much, and I was going to report him," the vampire paused to compose himself, "he threatened my precious pug. And now, they are both gone, and I may never see my sweet baby again."

With a few nods and silent direction, Mason instructed the other wardens to move forward on both Horatio and Raif. "Now that things are quieted down, let's all go back to the station. We need to figure out where Damien Mallory has gone and exactly what his involvement is."

I tugged on the detective's sleeve. "We don't have time for

official procedures. Raif, do you have any idea where he might be?"

Allowing a warden to escort him toward the door, he shook his head. "No. But, Miss Goodwin, if you can find him and my Sir Barklay, I will forever be in your debt."

The temptation of having something like that in my back pocket to keep the vampire from bugging me again interested me. But there were more important issues at hand than his selfish desires. I stood out of the way for the apprehensive wardens taking care of the troll to exit.

"You are smarter and supremely more talented than Holmes, Charli. Follow the path to its end," Horatio charged me.

While Mason and the rest of his team were busy handling things, I took the opportunity to snoop around, trying to find anything that might offer a clue to where Damien might have gone. A shimmering movement out of the corner of my eye captured my attention.

A rip in the space of Raif's parlor sparkled to life, and a hole opened. Moss, flew through it, hovering in front of the door. Behind her through the veil of the fairy path, I caught a glimpse of Blythe tied to a chair with a gag around her mouth, holding a terrified pug for dear life.

I opened my mouth to yell for Mason, but the small fairy held up a tiny finger in front of her lips. "One word from you, and I will close the path. The safety of your friend depends on the choices you make in the next few seconds."

Anger roared to life, and rage and power surged through

me. "What choices?" I gritted through my teeth, speaking low so no one else could hear me.

"Come with me willingly, and you can save her. Refuse and you risk your friend's life." Moss's normal sour face morphed into a more menacing mask.

"Those aren't choices," I hissed.

"You must decide now," insisted the fairy.

Keeping my eyes trained on Blythe and without looking back, I ran toward the shimmering door.

"Charli, no!" Mason screamed from behind. His protest trailed off as my feet landed on a rotten wooden floor and the portal closed.

Not taking in any of my surroundings, I rushed to kneel in front of my friend. "B, are you okay?" My fingers fumbled to check her body for injuries and to set her free. Blythe looked up at me, her eyes full of regret and dread.

A smooth voice with an impeccable British accent responded. "Your friend's safety and condition rests completely in your hands, Miss Goodwin. "

"Damien, what have you done to her?" Standing up, I prepared to face him with all of my wrath.

He ceased pretending to be the gentleman vampire, a sneering grin plastered on his face. "It is no longer what I did to her as much as what *you* choose to do for me that will determine her fate. And yours."

Chapter Twenty-Two

"Why don't you let me take care of the both of 'em?" snarled a large man, entering the room of the small abandoned house. I recognized Butch, one of Dash's attackers from the other night.

The vampire frowned, unhappy to be interrupted. "The two of you need to finish loading everything into the truck and depart. Moss's sleeping spell may not last long on the gate guard, and you need to be long gone to meet up with our contact on the outside." With a grunt, Butch shot me a dark gaze and left.

"So you're just a petty thief," I accused, my gut tightening. "Everything that happened was so you could steal things from our town? You murdered someone."

"I am far from a simple thief. What I do takes skills that few possess," bragged Damien. "The old woman was not as beneficial of a target as I had hoped. She provided the first domino in my deception, upsetting the election from the first event and providing an excellent cover for my real motives. But her mind would not allow her to fully accept my control. I had to stop her before she broke completely and alerted anyone to my game."

"A person's life is not a game." I rested my hand on Blythe's knee, giving her the comfort of my presence as she groaned and struggled against her bindings, Raif's dog whimpering in her grasp. "Did you influence her, too?"

He scoffed. "You witches continually underestimate others, creating communities to live in supposed harmony and expecting everyone to live by your rules and authority. I am a vampire, and we should not be living a less-than-ordinary life, trying to fit in with others. We were made to take lives."

Damien paced as he talked. "Sweet, simple Blythe here was a much easier target. So eager for someone to pay attention to her. Did you know that she is jealous of you because you hold two men's interests? It hardly drained me at all to manipulate her. Such interesting information she has, working that menial job and interacting with so many from your town."

Blythe shouted outraged words through her gag, struggling harder. If she broke free, the vampire would have a difficult time defending himself against both of us. I let a little power trickle down my arm to my fingertips, reaching my hand to touch the rope around her feet to free her.

"Stop right there, Charli." Damien placed a hand on

Blythe's shoulder, and she stopped fighting, her eyes clouding with an eerie calm. "No fair cheating when you are unaware of the rules. You haven't heard the *pièce de résistance* yet. Your part in all of this."

"What about my part?" The only advantage left to me was letting the man monologue for as long as possible until I could figure out a way to get me, my friend, and a dog out of here. Preferably still alive.

"It is a wonder you do not recognize me." He crouched down until his face rested in front of mine. "We crossed paths not that long ago. I had been taken in for questioning at a local warden station for suspicion of...other activities that are not relevant. When I was waiting to be processed, I overheard someone speaking to a young lady I was thrilled to discover possessed the very valuable abilities of tracking. This beautiful maiden spoke so warmly about her hometown with such affection that I couldn't help but visit the location." He reached out to touch me, and I flinched away. "I thank you for the suggestion. It has been most beneficial in more ways than I could have ever expected."

Blood rushed through me, and I almost collapsed under the weight of realization. I understood the nagging feeling that had plagued me when I was with him. A part of me had recognized seeing him at the station in my last days away from Honeysuckle. And because of me, so much had happened. I leaned on Blythe's lap for support, trying to keep the contents of my stomach from coming up.

Damien patted my head like he would an animal. "Don't

fret, dear girl. If you had recognized me, I could have used my influence on you to make you forget again. But I would rather not hold you in my thrall because it would benefit us both for you to choose to help me on your own."

Moss joined us, shooting me a dirty look and hovering possessively close to the vampire. I didn't hear their conversation, too wrapped up in my own guilt. "What have I done?" I moaned.

"Chin up. Being maudlin does not become you. The added bonus of discovering my old acquaintance living in this quaint backward town allows me to concoct an even bigger plan than a quick fleecing. Raif," Damien snorted. "The man liked to put on airs he didn't deserve even back then. You understand, that is not his name. I knew him as Baines. Bartholomew Baines. Old Barty was a mere porter and a complete *mumper* at the social club for my kind in Victorian London, always looking for a way to move up in the social chain. The Claret served as a perfect setting to hatch schemes and make connections, but anyone with the right motivation could garner precious information and use it to their advantage."

I didn't know if Damien spoke of himself or Raif, nor did I care. Whatever past the two vampires shared didn't help me at the moment. But the man enjoyed the sound of his voice enough to give me a chance to survey my surroundings. A broken chair lay on the floor so close that if I lunged for it, I could break the wood and get a piece sturdy enough to drive through the heart of the undead monster.

When Damien stood up, he grabbed me by my shirt,

dragging me upright and dashing my hopes of hurting him. "Enough talk. The boys will be finished loading the goods soon, and I will need to leave. So here is my offer. You come with me, and I will allow your friend and that blasted dog to remain alive."

"And if I don't," I challenged.

He sneered. "Then I will force you to come with me and kill them both. But I think you will accompany me. How could you not? There's a wide world out there ripe for the picking for someone with your talents. Do you not know that you could have riches beyond your wildest dreams? If people do not pay you to use your magic, then you can find and take what you want. You could afford a life much richer than the meager existence you settle for here, and it would be my honor to show you how." His eyes sparkled with passion, and he released me for a brief moment, caught up in his own reverie.

Taking my chance, I dove for the broken chair, the force of my body splintering it. My hand grasped the nearest fragment of wood and held onto it in a tight fist in front of me. "I like my life just fine, you arrogant unicorn's behind. There are more treasures here in Honeysuckle than you will ever understand."

Damien clapped his hands together. "Such spirit. I shall have to make sure not to dampen it too much when I compel you to leave. Hold her," he commanded a menacing presence behind me.

Strong muscles restrained me, and a rough grip forced the

wood out of my hand. I resisted, fighting back hard with kicks and twists, but my captor clasped me close. My elbow contacted his stomach, and the man cursed. "You should have just come with us," he grunted in my ear.

"Trey," I identified him. "I thought you promised Dash to leave town."

"I told that idiot what he needed to hear for him to leave us alone. It was an added bonus shattering his heart." He buried his nose in my neck and took a deep breath, scenting me from collarbone to ear. "I wonder if it would hurt him more to know that I had you right now."

"He means nothing to me," I lied.

Trey snorted. "Sure. That's why you listened in on our conversation in the alley. Not too smart, hanging around angry wolf shifters." He brought his hand to my neck and squeezed. "A girl could get herself hurt."

"Enough," barked Damien. "She is not to be harmed, do you understand?"

Trey's growl vibrated in his chest. "Then finish things and let's go."

Butch stood in the front doorway, and Damien addressed him. "Since Miss Charli chooses not to come willingly, then I need you to take care of them." He pointed at Blythe and Raif's dog.

I writhed in protest, building up a charge of power in my center and blasting the crackling hex through my body. It zapped Trey who dropped me with a bark of surprise. Rushing to Blythe, I used what sparks I had left in me to do away with the ropes holding her. I set Sir Barklay on the floor, and yelled at him to run, watching his tiny body dodge the two shifters and escape into the night.

The room erupted into chaos. One second, Butch snarled at me and coiled his body, ready to spring on me. The next, a hulking form tackled him and threw him on the floor, beating and punching him until he stopped moving.

"Get outta here, Charli," Dash ordered. "Now."

"Not without Blythe," I called out. Putting my arm around my friend's shoulders, I attempted to lift her up, but Trey got to me first. He picked me up in his arms, holding me tighter than before, and I struggled to breathe.

"Back off, Dash, or I will hurt her," he warned.

Both Damien and my wolf shifter attempted to plead with him. Trey backed away with me in tow. "This couldn't have worked out more perfectly. First, I can take all the goods myself since Sir Vampy here values *your* life so much," he explained in my ear. "And as an added bonus, I can finally get my revenge on you, Dash."

"Why?" Dash growled.

"Remember when I told you about Dina? How she was doing okay in college? It was all a lie. The Red Ridge pack has her captive, and your brother forces me to pay him every month to keep her safe, as if I don't know that he'll take what he wants in the long run. But *you*...you hide out here and think you're sheltered from it all, ignoring the destruction you left behind. Well, how about I destroy something you value while you watch it being taken away from you?" He strangled me with one hand, his fingers curling tighter, my gasps growing short and loud.

"Trey, stop. Don't do this," pleaded Dash, looking on in helpless conflict.

"And what did you do when we all begged you not to go? You didn't listen either. I hope her death tears you apart," Trey snarled, squeezing. The world faded away and darkened.

In desperation, Damien cried out, "No. Moss, contingency plan. Now!"

The fairy who'd been hovering on the perimeter of the room, spun in tight circles, gray-green dust spiraling off her wings. A glow pulsed around her small body, and with a shriek, she exploded, hurdling power at all of us.

The old structure disappeared, and I collapsed on the ground of dirt and tufts of grass, gasping for air. When I got my bearings, I recognized the thick twisting branches hung with Spanish moss of the Founders' tree with the last rays of the sun radiating through the lush canopy.

"What are we doing here?" I choked out, rubbing my neck from the pain.

Damien crouched next to Moss who lay on the ground as still as a stone. "This is my last bet to place. My ace in the hole. You said I did not appreciate your town's riches, but you are mistaken. I need you to help me locate the treasure buried here. I will take it and you with me." He still held enough threat in his tone to worry me.

"I don't think you get it. The treasures that Blythe told you about aren't exactly what you think." I thought back on the last Founders' Day events, wondering what value the vampire would place on my late parents' simple gold wedding bands or any of the other things each of the founding representatives used to cast the protective spell on our town.

"Then help me find them and let me be the judge of their worth," he replied, attempting to scare me with a flash of his sharp fangs. "I may have lost my hired muscle, but do not take my own strength for granted."

Fearing what might happen if he took away even one of the foundational treasures, I stood firm. "There's nothing you can do or say to make me help you."

His lips widened in a pompous smile. "Oh, I think you will." He dug into his suit pocket and pulled out a folded paper, waving it in the air. "This will ensure your compliance." He took a step forward. "You know how you were having the cleaning company sift through your papers? I am sure you were looking for something in particular. Time to find the treasures or say goodbye to your one chance at finding out who you really are."

A battle raged inside me. The idea of possessing that first clue to my relatives and my magic had become my secret obsession since Tipper's death. Knowing that a possible answer was so close made me question everything.

Damien pushed harder. "Do you know why those with your magical talents are rare? Because a few of your kind switched sides, choosing to use their powers to work with humans to hunt other magical beings down for nothing more than sport and wealth. Countless deaths littered the world due to hunters and trackers much like yourself. Tracker bloodlines of the guilty and the innocent alike were annihilated until only a few survived, going into hiding until the past was forgotten. Is it not an intriguing mystery to solve, whether or not you descend from traitors or the honorable who fought to survive? Help me, and the knowledge is yours," he offered.

Others like me had made choices that cost lives, demolishing them in their wake and causing the destruction of entire family lines. And what about *my* family here in Honeysuckle? Not just Nana and Matt, but TJ and my niece to come, all of my friends...Mason and Dash. Was solving the mystery of my past worth destroying their futures?

My decision made, I crossed my arms. "Do what you want with the information. I still refuse."

The paper crinkled in his hand, and Damien grunted in frustration, unable to follow through with his threat. "Your life is still not your own. I will tell those who employ me about you, and they will come and find you. They could destroy the entire town and take you in a single visit. As I said, talents like yours are rare and prized. If you won't volunteer to use them, there are ways to force you that are less than pleasant. "

Behind the vampire, Moss blinked and sat up, still groggy from her burst of power. A last-ditch plan dawned on me. "You used Moss to find my adoption papers, didn't you? I'm surprised you would stoop so low as to rely on someone like her."

Damien sniffed. "I never knew how convenient fairies could be. They do have a knack for getting in and out without detection if they are properly motivated. So simple. So elegant, and almost impossible to track, as you proved."

"Did you compel her like you did Mrs. Kettlefields or Blythe?" I asked, watching Moss catch up to the conversation.

The vampire snorted. "No need to waste valuable energy on her. A few romantic overtures and she took the bait of my affections, becoming a willing participant. In fact, it was her idea to take what she had discovered at your house. The little thing proved to be quite useful in landing me the one thing I really wanted. You." He shook the paper in his hand. "Give in, Charli."

He never saw it coming. Moss fluttered to life, expending what magic she had left to blast him from behind and knock him down. "You said you wanted *me*," she accused in her squeaky voice. "That she was inconsequential. A tool to be used."

Damien grunted on the ground a foot away from where she collapsed again. "It takes one to know one, my dear." He recovered, standing up and dusting himself off. "But now, I fear our time together has come to an end, as has your usefulness." With a quick hand, he snatched her up by the throat. Looking at me instead of her, he spoke with wicked intention. "I take lives." Moss's wings dropped, and her body went limp.

What did I have left to fight him? With little effort, he could put me in his thrall and make me obey his every command, and then I would be lost forever. Or if I fought hard enough, perhaps he would end my life like the fairy's. A sad resignation weighed on me. Either way, life as I knew it would be over.

Insistent caws echoed through the evening air. A dark figure circled the tree until it settled on a branch not too far away. Biddy squawked at me, arriving to witness my end. She pecked at the bark underneath her talons, hopping on the limb in agitation.

"Fly away, you bird. Get out of that tree." Damien waved his hands, distracted.

The tree. Biddy wanted me to notice where we stood. The giant live oak served as the beacon of power for our town. Power pulsed through it at all times, protecting every single being who chose to live here. If I could tap into that magic, I might be able to boost a hexing spell and at least stun Damien.

Knowing my spellcasting limitations, in desperation, I added the one thing I needed to give me focus. "*The vampire wants to win his bet, by putting me and mine at threat. Give me magic to end his time, and stop him from his life of crime. So pretty please with sweet iced tea, to save the town, bring power to me.*"

The tree hummed to life around us. A light shimmered and glowed, and a power unknown to me spread from the bottoms of my feet and up my legs, pulsing through my veins. All doubt vanished, and I gave in to the crest of magic filling me to the brim.

"What are you doing?" Damien cried.

"Making sure you do no harm to those who live here. Tonight, I act as the town's protector." Sparks crackled over my entire body.

Holding up the paper in both his hands as if to tear it, he countered in distress, all of his bluster gone. "If something happens to me, then you can say goodbye to this."

I tilted my head at his empty threat. With a flick of my fingers, the folded paper caught fire in his hand. He dropped the smoldering remains on the ground, backing away from the blaze and cowering like cornered prey. If I could do that to the paper, what could I do to him?

"Spare me, I beg of you," he pleaded.

The noise of several people joining us filled the air, but I kept my eyes trained on Damien, not willing to let him go. A large wolf sauntered to my side and bumped my hip, its lips pulling back in a fierce snarl.

"I've got this, Dash," I said.

Mason joined me on my other side. "But you don't have to do it alone, and I need to take him in. He has more things to answer for than the chaos he brought to our town. Please, Charli. I can't allow you to destroy him." The detective ignored the roar of protest from Dash.

Sensing his nearing defeat, Damien straightened and confronted those of us who could hear him. "You are all fools, hiding away from the rest of the world. Your lives will amount to nothing," he spit out in defiance.

The tree pulsed again, and my magic surged. "Aw, bless

your heart," I gathered the power from my body into my hands and focused it, "and hex your whiny hiney."

With a mighty cry, I directed everything in me at the vampire. Magic poured out of my body until nothing remained. A steady hand gripped me, anchoring my efforts and pulling me back into myself. Exhausted and spent, I slumped over, a furry body breaking my fall before I slipped to the bottom of a deep well of darkness.

Chapter Twenty-Three

I opened my eyes to the worst sight in the world. A tall glass full of gray sludge floated in front of my face. Whipping the quilt back over my head, I rolled over and shuddered.

"Charli Bird, you've got to stop makin' it a habit of gettin' yourself into trouble." Nana sat down on the edge of the bed, the mattress dipping next to me. She patted my behind covered by the blanket. "Come on. No use hidin' under there. There's things you have to do, and I can't keep them at bay for much longer."

With caution, I pulled the quilt off me. "Who's waiting for me?"

"When you attack a wanted international criminal and almost take him out, you tend to attract all kinds of attention." She shoved the glass in my face, the stench of it turning my stomach. "Drink all of this down, and then make yourself presentable. The detective will be bringing the other guests by in a hot minute."

I groaned and attempted to hide again, but Nana held onto the blanket, preventing me. She stroked my hair. "Get up, sweetness. Morning's here to greet you with her shining light."

My heart warmed at our old wake-up game. "Nobody here but us chickens," I joked.

Cupping my chin, my grandmother gazed at me with fierce love. "And I am mighty glad this bird did not fly to the great beyond last night, even when she put her own life at risk for the rest of us." Her eyes pooled with wetness, and we both shed tears of relief and thankfulness.

When our sniffling stopped long enough, I swung my feet out of bed. "Okay, okay, I'm up."

"Good." Nana wrapped me up in a quick hug and released me. "Get yourself clean, dressed, and fed. You'll wanna fuel up before the guests arrive." She headed out the door, but before she got to the bottom of the stairs, she yelled back up, "And you better bring an empty glass down with you. You know I'll know if you don't drink it all."

It was tempting to pour the contents down the drain of the shower, but Nana definitely would figure it out, so I endured the nasty stuff, wondering if there would ever come a day when I wouldn't have to drink it in the first place. About the time I finished a second helping of scrambled eggs with onion and ham mixed in, someone rapped on the screen door.

"Ms. Vivi, is she finally up?" our town's sheriff called out from the front porch.

Nana glanced at me. "Better pull on your big girl britches. When you get through everything, I'll give you the biggest slice of chess pie you've ever seen." She left to greet whoever waited with the sheriff.

Downing the rest of my coffee and finishing off the last crumbly bite of my cheesy buttermilk biscuit, I shoved myself away from the old kitchen table.

"I'll help you get the tea, Ms. Goodwin," Mason called out, on his way to the kitchen. He pushed the swing door open and froze when he saw me. "Charli. You're looking better than I expected."

"Thanks?" I hated it when a compliment sounded more like an insult.

He entered the room, attempting a couple of times to correct himself before giving up with a sigh. "I meant, I'm glad to see you. After the other night, I wasn't sure how you would be."

I frowned. "How long was I out?"

"Your grandmother didn't tell you?"

I shook my head, a little bit of worry creeping in. "It's been that long?"

He counted on his fingers. "Three nights and two days. We've been forced to come by every day to see if you were ready."

"You and Big Willie?" Confused, I sat back down.

Mason scratched the back of his head. "A few more than

that. It's been hard putting them off, but seeing as you're the most important part of the investigation, they had to wait."

My eyes darted toward the back door. "Any chance you'd let me make a run for it?"

He chuckled. "Only if you took me with you." His burning gaze suggested there might be some truth to his words. "Come on. I'll be right there by your side, and it will be over before you know it." The detective held out his hand to help me up.

I accepted his assistance and relished his warm touch. He pulled me upward, my body launching into his. For a brief moment, nothing else existed.

Nana cleared her throat. "If you two are quite finished, they're waiting for you in there. I'll bring out the tea, Detective." Her eyes twinkled with mirth at my burning cheeks when we passed her.

Mason escorted me to the parlor, and I stopped in the doorway. Three other people occupied the available seats while one hovered near the sofa. Their eyes snapped in my direction, and I tried not to squirm under their scrutiny.

As a tall Sasquatch unable to fit in any of our seating comfortably, Big Willie stood on the other side of the room. He waved his hairy hand at me, and nodded with purpose at Mason.

The detective cleared his throat. "I think the first thing we need to do is make some introductions. Everybody, this is Charlotte Goodwin. Charli, let me introduce these two first." He gestured at the man and woman sitting in adjoining chairs.

"This is Chief Investigator Lilith Marsden and her colleague, Deputy Investigator Thomas Pine. They're from the World Organization of Wardens."

"Pleased to finally meet you, Miss Goodwin," the female investigator replied in a stiff tone.

I shook her hand. "Wow."

"What? Surprised that a female witch could make it this far up the chain?" she asked. Based on her quick reaction, she'd faced her challenges getting where she was.

"Oh, no. Sorry, I just meant that you work for *WOW*. Not wow, I can't believe you're a girl." I stumbled. "A woman, not a girl, although you don't look old either. I am just swallowin' my foot whole, aren't I?"

Nana joined us, handing me a glass of tea from the tray she carried. "Here, put some of this in your mouth and see if it clears it out." She passed around the rest of the drinks. "My granddaughter is more than used to seeing a woman in charge, considering I occupy the highest seat in our town council. Now, let's move things along, shall we?"

Mason stepped forward again. "These two are working in cooperation with Agent Dryope of the International Magic Patrol."

The stoic countenance of the tall, willowy woman with light green hair prevented me from commenting on what the initials of her organization spelled. "Pleasure to meet you, Agent Dryope."

She shook my hand with the lightest touch. "It's pronounced like Calliope," she corrected. "And as you're staring at the leaves in my hair, I will inform you that I'm a dryad."

If I could have summoned a hole in the ground to jump in, I would have.

"And this is Agent Giacinta," finished Mason, ducking out of the room at the end of his introductions.

"*Con piacere*." The beautiful fairy replied in a high-pitched lilting accent, her wings flickering a light purple dust with her greeting. "Our many thanks to you and your *nonna* for hosting us in your fine home."

"It is most unusual to hold an interrogation in one's domicile." Agent Dryope flicked a strand of leaves from her face. "But I suppose, given the circumstances, we can make do."

"Interrogation?" I asked, overwhelmed by everything.

Mason reappeared, carrying a dining room chair. He placed it down for me to sit. "We need you to fill everybody in on what happened from the first night of the election speeches to the last thing you can remember."

Placing my exhausted behind on the cushion, I did my best to recall all the details. The four strangers took notes and clarified when needed, seeming to be familiar with most of the timeline. Once I got going, the information poured out of me, and my hands gesticulated in the air while I told my story.

When I got to the part of figuring out that having the stolen goods in the presence of a vampire or even a fairy blocked my magical talents, I clapped my hand over my mouth, suddenly realizing that I might have shared too much.

Damien's voice echoed in my head, warning me that others outside of my town would be interested in what I could do.

"*Non ti preoccupare, bella*," reassured Agent Giacinta. "What you say here to us is strictly for our files. You need have no worries that your information shall be shared outside of here."

"Although, having a tracker on hand would come in handy," the female warden investigator commented, her colleague nodding and eyeing me with too much interest.

Agent Dryope shook her leafy head. "Let us remain focused on the issue at hand. Tell us about what Damien Mallory said to you when you confronted him."

I held up my finger. "Hold on. What happened to Blythe?" I couldn't believe I had forgotten to ask about my friend.

Nana touched my shoulder. "She's doing better. After Raif got his precious dog back, he sent word to Lady Eveline to return home. I guess she has some experience in helping those who have been...influenced by someone like Damien. She got back yesterday, and is already working with Blythe."

I'd have to stop by to check on my friend soon. I hated that she'd gone through that entire experience. The memory of how Damien had come to Honeysuckle trickled back into my brain, and I slumped forward. Regret penetrated all the cracks and crevices of my spirit, and I confessed the truth to Nana, aware that the others heard it and added my guilt to their notes.

Inspector Mallory uncrossed her legs. "Miss Goodwin, we're aware of his involvement in the investigation in Greenville as well as the person you were working with at the time. You did not drag him to your town. He made that choice for himself along with continuing his life of crime." She nodded at me, and I appreciated her attempt to ease my conscience.

Wanting to get things over with, I sped through the stuff that happened in the abandoned broken down house and got to the Founders' tree. The image of Moss's last breaths sent shivers down my body. Agent Giacinta's wings quivered in agitation, and I wondered how unbiased she could remain, knowing that one of her kind was involved.

"This misuse of the fairy path. It is a problem in your town, no?" she asked.

I shrugged. "It's not like that's how we all move around. For the most part, the fairies don't use it." I didn't want to have to admit how many times *I* had taken the shortcut or who had provided it for me the most. Gossamer had enough on her plate to deal with.

"Still, perhaps you might want to discuss it with your local fairy folk. It is not a typical privilege given to others, and it can have effects on those who abuse it that are more dangerous than you think," she added.

"Hey, how did you find me that night?" I asked Mason, avoiding the accusatory glance from the fairy agent.

"Spell phone," he replied with a slight grin.

"How?" My own device had fried before then.

"I slipped mine in your back pocket when you were talking to Raif and Horatio." He lifted his left eyebrow at me, and I recalled the light pat of my behind with an audible gasp. Sneaky detective.

Deputy Inspector Pine took a bigger phone with a screen on it out of his pocket. "How are cell phones working here? Mine won't even power up."

I shook my head. "We have *spell* phones. One of my friends here spellworked old flip phones to work off of our power rather than having a system that tries to combine magic with human electricity like you have out there."

"A magic-only device for communicating. That's pretty ingenious. I'd like to know who provided this for you before we leave," he said in awe. "We might be able to make him a deal."

Nana replaced my empty glass with the rest of her iced tea. "Ladies and gents, if we could finish, my granddaughter needs to rest and recover."

When I told the part about Damien's possession of my adoption papers, I couldn't look at my grandmother, afraid that she might think my desire to know about my past meant I was rejecting our family. The fact that I burned the paper voluntarily impressed all of the magical authority sitting in the room.

Nana kissed the top of my head. "Sweet bird, you have no idea how proud I am of you. If there's something you want to find out there, I will do everything I can to help you. And no piece of paper determines whether or not you're my granddaughter. There's no way you're gettin' rid of me."

"Also, Damien Mallory was a con artist," filled in Agent

Dryope. "There is a good chance that what he had was nothing. Maybe even blank."

"*Was?* Did I...did I kill him?" The pit in my stomach expanded into a canyon.

"No," Mason replied before the others. "He's being detained down at the station."

"He's annoying everyone there, always askin' us where he is, what his name is, what time it is," added Big Willie. "The poor fool seems to have a problem in his noggin'."

"Yes," sniffed Agent Dryope. "The power you wielded that night affected both of you, it seems. You managed to wipe out his entire memory, which is a great inconvenience to us as he could have been an important lynchpin in taking down other organizations. In addition," she turned to my grandmother, "I still advise that your granddaughter accompany us back to one of our facilities. An uncontrolled amount of magic like that should not go unchecked."

Anxiety gathered in my chest. "I feel fine," I protested.

"She is being cared for quite thoroughly, I'll have you know," Nana huffed.

"No offense, ma'am, but the agent is right," chimed in Deputy Pine. "There are better facilities which could handle her right now."

My heart raced, and a tingling sensation crawled over my skin. "I'm not leaving Honeysuckle."

"Charli," Mason said, approaching my chair.

"No. There's nothing wrong with me," I insisted. "They can't take me away from here. They can't!" I shouted. All of the glasses shattered at the same time, splashing brown liquid everywhere.

Sweet honeysuckle iced tea, what was happening to me? I stared at my body, scared down to my bones. Because *I* had done that.

"That right there." Agent Dryope stood, wiping her hands down her moistened clothes. "That is precisely why she should not stay in your town. She could be a danger to you all if she channeled as much magic as you suggest that she did from your tree."

Nana faced off with the agent. "It'll probably take some time. She's like a light bulb that's had a little too much juice sent to her wires. She'll burn bright for a while, but eventually, she'll calm down."

"Or she'll burst, and no telling how big that explosion might get." The agent's green leaves rustled with her irritation.

"Now, now, everybody needs to calm down. Nobody's takin' anybody anywhere." Big Willie held up his hairy arms. "In my personal opinion, it'll take fillin' her belly with some good ol' down home cookin' to work things out. Y'all should stay and try out some of our real good food here. I'm tellin' you, it's the best medicine in all the world. In the meantime, how 'bout we promise that if things start goin' wonky with Miss Charli that we'll contact you?" He ushered the four magical authorities toward the door.

Chief Inspector Marsden slipped a business card to me. "If you ever want to consider taking a job with our department, let me know. Tracker abilities are very desirable. Thank you for your time."

Agent Giacinta hovered on the porch, waiting for the rest to head to their vehicles. "*Signorina* Charli, if I may call you that."

"Sure." Something about the fairy put me at immediate ease.

"I do not want you to think that we are all as serious as my fellow agent. There are many of us who enjoy visiting new places and meeting new people despite the reasons why we go. You did well, dealing with Damien, and although Agent Dryope sees the outcome as...how you say...inconvenient to her, I believe that having his memory wiped may be beneficial to you, your town, and any others he would have hurt in the future."

"I appreciate you saying that." I shook her tiny hand.

She tilted her head. "Do not let fear dictate your life. *Sì,* your magic may have value to others, but you hold your destiny in your own hands. If I had the choice to stay in such a place as this, I am not sure I would want to leave either, no?" she finished in her attractive accent.

I nodded, happy to have someone who understood me so quickly. "Agent Giacinta, before you leave, make sure you have the fried chicken plate at the Harvest Moon Cafe and a slice of red velvet cake at Sweet Tooths. Tell them to put it all on my tab."

The fairy flitted to me and kissed me on both cheeks.

"*Grazie*, Charli. May our paths cross again, but hopefully not for the same reason."

"And not on the fairy path," I joked.

She tittered, a little purple dust floating off her. "*Ciao*." With a wave, she flew off.

Nana walked back up the steps of the porch, watching the outsiders leave. "They're going to the station to pick up Damien and take him away. Now that everything's solved, I guess someone's gonna have to plan Eugenia's parting party. Just because she doesn't have any children doesn't mean she's not one of us."

I put my arm around my grandmother. "Mrs. K had lots of kids. Leave it to me. I'll put out the word, and by the time I'm done, she'll have a parting party like no other. I'm thinkin' a huge pig pickin'. That woman loved her barbecue."

"Sounds good to me, Birdy," chuckled Nana. "Now, how 'bout I cut you the biggest slice of some chess pie. I think you've earned it."

Epilogue

Nana had almost called off the entire election due to the murder, the planted evidence, the almost-arrests, and the coverage in the newspaper. Since Linsey was responsible for most of the scandal that disrupted things, my grandmother convinced her to stick to the facts and stop stirring the pot or else. Having been on the other side of Nana's *or else*'s before, I'd bet Linsey would stay on the straight and narrow for a while.

Mrs. Eugenia Kettlefields had a parting party like no other. Many of her former students who had left Honeysuckle returned home to pay their respects and eat some good barbecue with all the fixings. Thanks to Lee and a few others who dug around in her past, they found out a lot more about her and shared her life with others so that we could appreciate the woman who considered all of us her kids.

Although we were too late in life to express our thanks in person, we made sure to send them to her wherever she rested now.

Tonight, Jordy and the Jack-O'-Lanterns played on stage while the whole town ate good food. Several people had hot grills going, and the smell of sizzling meat filled the air. Plates and dishes stuffed with casseroles and homemade goods covered table upon table, and the sweet tea flowed like a river. A large banner congratulating the election winner floated in the air above the gazebo stage. Nearby, Goss hovered close, decorating everything she could in pink to celebrate her husband's victory. Pride swelled in my chest for my friends.

"Where can I put this?" Mason called out to me.

I turned and spotted a foil container with something slightly brown and off-putting in it. "First, identify what it is."

"It's lasagna," he said, frowning at the contents. "I made it."

"Oh." I pursed my lips to keep from laughing. "I suggest that you put it over there, then."

"You're pointing at that trash can."

"Exactly."

"Brat." Mason glanced down at his creation and over to where my finger directed him. "But you're right. This is most likely inedible." Walking over, he tossed it in the bin.

"Still, I'm impressed with your efforts, Detective," I teased.

"I'm trying. Seems that food is an important part of living in this town. I can't keep mooching off others. I'll have to eventually pick a good dish to bring to these things and learn how to actually make it." He smiled with a sheepish grin. "I'm good at a lot of things, but cooking doesn't seem to be one of them."

I slipped my arm through his and led him in the direction of the real food. "It just takes practice. I'll help."

"I look forward to the lessons, Miss Goodwin." He put his hand over mine that held onto his arm, squeezing it.

I spotted Dash heading our way, balancing two large dishes of what looked like his fried chicken on them. Letting Mason go, I went to help, clearing off a large area on one of the tables. "You fried up all this?"

He shrugged. "It's nothing. The least I can do to contribute since I'm tryin' to be a good town citizen and participate."

My cheeks heated under his intense gaze, my heart beating harder than the drummer on the stage. "I think that's a good start."

"Although I'll be leavin' Honeysuckle for a while," he added, watching me carefully.

My stomach dropped. "What? When?" I hadn't spoken to Dash since he'd shown up at my side in his wolf form, not even taking the chance to give him my thanks for standing by me or telling him how glad I was that he was a much better man than Trey or Butch.

"In the morning. I've got my bike's saddlebags already packed and ready to go." He touched my arm. "But I wanted to come here tonight."

"To celebrate with Flint. I think we're all happy he was the only one left after everyone else refused to get back in the race. Honestly, I think he would have had the majority's vote anyway." If I kept the wolf shifter talking, would I be able to convince him not to go?

"I'm happy for the gnome. But I came here tonight to talk to you." Weaving his fingers through mine, he walked me away from the crowd. I glanced back and caught Mason watching us find some privacy.

Dash took me to a bench and offered to let me sit. I shook my head, needing to stand as close as face to face as possible. He kept my hand in his. "I feel like I'm always screwing things up. And then I have to apologize to you."

Remembering our motorcycle ride together, I smiled. "But sometimes your apologies are fun."

He grunted, but his lip twitched a little. "I'd love to take you on rides every single day if I could. Having your body wrapped tight around mine," he whistled. "That's a fantasy I never thought would come true." The heat in his eyes hinted at his double meaning.

"Then stay," I whispered.

His expression filled with a dark shadow. "I can't. I meant it when I said I was no good."

"Dash, don't start—"

"Shh." He held a finger to my lips. "Let me finish. I don't talk about my past because there are some bad things there. Awful, horrific things that should never touch you. You only got a glimpse of them that night you watched Trey and me in the alley."

"I hope you kicked his rotten behind into the ground," I gritted through my teeth, wishing the other shifter as much ill will as possible.

"I could have killed him for threatening your life."

"But you didn't," I said, hoping that the words were true.

"No. Mason made sure to transfer him to the jail up near where my old pack is. I don't know where Butch was sent." He looked away into the sky at a dark bird circling in the late afternoon sun. "I have to go back to Red Ridge."

Concern for the man in front of me possessed every atom of my being. "But from what Trey said, it's horrible there."

"And that's my doin'. I left there, thinking things would be better. It's my brother that's makin' things worse. I'm the oldest, so it's my job to fix things. And who knows, maybe Trey was lying."

We both knew the other shifter spoke the truth. He had too much venom in him. "If you leave, how long will you be gone?"

Dash sighed. "I don't know. If I can get some help from a few others up there, it might not be that hard to oust Cash."

My lower lip trembled, and I looked down, not wanting him to see the tears pooling in my eyes. "What if they want you to stay and be their alpha?" I held back the real question I wanted to ask him. *What if you don't come back?*

He furrowed his brow. "I can't think that far ahead. I have to focus on the first step." Glancing at me, he softened and cupped my cheek. "Besides, I've promised to fix Old Joe. And that's one thing I'm not gonna screw up."

His thumb caressed my cheek, and he leaned in, his hot breath warming the sensitive skin of my mouth. I closed my eyes, anticipating one of my late night dreams coming true, my heart threatening to leap out of my chest.

With a slight groan, Dash tilted my head down and planted his warm lips on my forehead. "Oh, Charli."

I threw my arms around him, wanting to hold him here, protect him, and make him see himself through my eyes rather than through his all at the same time.

Dash buried his face in my hair, drawing in long breaths. He ran his nose down my jawline and across my cheek until he found my nose, rubbing his against mine in a sensual greeting. Taking his time to inhale, he pulled back my hair to expose my neck and dragged his face up and down my neck, sending hot chills down to my belly.

"Are you scenting me?" I tried my best to stay upright despite the tremble in my legs.

He nodded, his beard tickling my skin.

"So that you'll remember me if you don't come back?" I feared.

Dash pulled away, placing both his hands on my cheeks. "No. So that the essence of you will call me back home." He gave me one last chaste peck on my forehead. "Maybe I should go now before I get caught up in the one reason I want to stay."

He didn't say anything more, and I let him release me and

walk away. I couldn't watch him go, and I didn't want anybody to see me cry over his decision. Collapsing on the nearby bench, I gave in to my confused emotions.

Biddy announced her presence with a caw and landed next to me. She hopped up on my lap and flapped her way onto my shoulder. I loved how she always knew, and took comfort in her presence, sitting for a moment together on the bench in silent support.

"Hey, girl, would you mind following him out of town?" I didn't know why I wanted her to or what peace of mind it would give me. But if I couldn't watch his departure, somebody I cared about could.

She nodded her dark head and cocked it to regard me. With another caw, the crow took off into the sky. I wiped my eyes of any evidence of tears and headed back to join my friends.

All my girls, including Blythe, met me at the edge. I nodded at my friend who still acted more fragile than I'd ever seen her.

Lavender stared at the air around me, no doubt interpreting my aura. Her cousin Lily touched my arm. "Everything okay?"

I nodded, marveling at their undying support. "Yeah. How did y'all know?"

"Mason sent us to find you," Blythe replied, holding out a cup no doubt filled with iced tea. "Said you might need us."

"And at least one slice of chess pie." Alison Kate held out a plate and fork to me.

I accepted the pie, the tea, and their love, appreciating the detective's ability to make sure I had things I didn't even know I needed. He stayed on the other side of the crowd, deep in conversation with Lee. But his protective glances never wavered for the rest of the night, and I was glad that the wall of ice that he'd erected between us was finally melted and gone. What would the future hold for the two of us if nothing stood in the way? More emotions whirled inside me, and I gulped down sweet tea to help.

Horatio approached with Juniper close at hand. The betrayal of Moss and her death weighed on the tiny fairy who seemed more reserved than ever except in the troll's presence.

"My dear Charli. Allow me to extend my congratulations for following the clues to the end and solving the mystery. Well done, Holmes." Horatio clapped me on the back, knocking the breath out of me.

"I don't think I deserve that name, but thanks."

He handed me a small rectangular card, and I turned it over in my hand. In precise handwritten calligraphy, it read:

Charli Goodwin

Lost & Found Services

For there is nothing lost, that may be found, if sought.

Fees to be determined on case basis

"Where's the quote from?" I asked.

Horatio smiled. "Edmund Spenser, from his epic poem, *The Faerie Queene*. I thought it very appropriate."

I stared at the card and read it over again. "You know, I'm not opening a business, right?"

Both he and Juniper chuckled. The troll patted my head. "With every case that you solve, your renown will grow. Already there are stirrings of people willing to pay for your assistance. Do not dismiss the opportunity lightly nor close the door when Fate comes knocking." With a wave, they both left to greet others who were appreciative of the way both ex-candidates had contributed to tonight's victory.

I stood at the back of the crowd, half-listening to the council speeches and half-tangled up in my own emotions. Unbeknownst to my friends, the effects of drawing on the magic from the tree still lingered. No telling how the extra boost would affect my magic, and frankly, I wasn't ready to find out yet.

And there I stood in the middle of it all—A town that I loved. Friends and family that I would die for. A man that pushed my intellect and made me better in so many ways. And another man who just rode a motorcycle out of town, taking my wilder side with him.

Shaking myself out of my head, I tried to pay attention to Flint as started his acceptance speech. I agreed with him, that only when we banded together as a community would we be strong and worthy of the little slice of paradise we'd cooked up here in our small Southern town.

I started to lift my cup to toast the gnome's sentiments and found it empty. Focusing on what I wanted and feeling the buzz of magic in my veins, I snapped my fingers. Sweet iced tea with the floral scent of honeysuckle filled the red plastic to the top. What other spells were just waiting to be discovered inside of me?

Lifting my glass, I toasted with everyone else. "To our future."

❦

DEAR READER -

Thanks so much for reading *Fried Chicken & Fangs*. If you enjoyed the book (as much as I did writing it), I hope you'll consider leaving a review!

NEWSLETTER ONLY - If you want to be notified when the next story is released and to get access to exclusive content, sign up for my newsletter! https://www.subscribepage.com/t4v5z6

NEWSLETTER & FREE PREQUEL - to gain exclusive access to the prequel *Chess Pie & Choices*, go here! https://dl.bookfunnel.com/opbg5ghpyb

Southern Charms Cozy Mystery Series

Magic & Mystery are only part of the Southern Charms of Honeysuckle Hollow...

Suggested reading order:

Chess Pie & Choices: A Southern Charms Cozy Prequel

(Available exclusively to Newsletter Subscribers)

Charli Goodwin is engaged to Tucker Hawthorne, the admired "prince" of Honeysuckle Hollow. Underneath the perfect surface of their union boils an ocean of doubt. If he's such a catch, then why does she feel like she's on the hook?

When Charli's magical talents are put to the test to find something valuable to Tucker's family, she's set on a path that will test her love and show her where her true *happy ever after* may be.

Moonshine & Magic: A Southern Charms Cozy Mystery Book 1

Charli Goodwin doesn't expect her homecoming to go without a hitch—after all, she skipped town, leaving her fiancé and family without a clue as to where she was going or why. Now that she's ready to return home, she plans to lay low and sip some of her Nana's sweet tea while the town gossips come out to play.

Unfortunately, on her first night back, Charli discovers the body of her crazy great uncle (hey, everyone has one). She suddenly finds herself at the center of a mystery that threatens the very foundations of Honeysuckle Hollow and the safety of every paranormal citizen in it—starting with Charlie herself.

With the clock ticking, will Charli's special magical talents be enough to save not only the town but her own life?

Lemonade & Love Potions (a short formerly included in the anthology *Hexes & Ohs*)

Charli Goodwin can't help herself when it comes to helping out her friends, especially a failed cupid trying to earn his way back into the matchmaking ranks. A singles mingle in her small Southern town should be the perfect event, but trouble with a capital *T* shows up when someone attempts to boost the odds of love in their favor.

Sweet honeysuckle iced tea, it's gonna take more than lemonade and a little magic to help Charli find out what's wrong, solve the mystery, and save Honeysuckle Hollow from disaster again.

Fried Chicken & Fangs: A Southern Charms Cozy Mystery Book 2

An upcoming election shakes up Honeysuckle. When an outspoken resident who opposes the changes to the magical small Southern town turns up dead, it's up to Charli Goodwin and her special talents to get on the case...except her valuable magic doesn't seem to be working.

What starts as a simple search uncovers a darker layer of manipulation and sabotage. Will Charli be able to figure out who is pulling the strings before the foundations of the town are destroyed?

Sweet Tea & Spells: A Southern Charms Cozy Mystery Book 3

With her ex-fiancé's wedding to her cousin on the horizon, Charli Goodwin has to be on her best behavior. But when an outsider infiltrates Honeysuckle, another murder threatens to ruin more than just the future of the upcoming nuptials.

At the same time, wolf shifter Dash Channing is gone and a changed Detective Mason Clairmont makes a new declaration. Will Charli be able to cast her personal feelings aside to break all the rules and help capture the real killer or will more trouble be heading to the small supernatural Southern town?

Barbecue & Brooms: A Southern Charms Cozy Mystery Book 4 (Coming Soon)

Acknowledgments

I'm grateful for the consistent support I received while writing this book from family and friends to fellow authors. I'd like to give credit to a few who, without them, I might not have gotten to the end.

My Tiki group, you are the first I go to and the last I check with. Thanks for putting up with me.

Mel, "Melanie Summers", thank you for being the upbeat person that you are and my constant cheerleader. Without our conversations, the page might still be blank.

Alana, you not only provided me with laughs but also you will forever be my permanent movie date and breakfast companion.

Many thanks go to ReGina Welling, who checked in on me every day.

To Annabel Chase and Amanda Lee, my two friends and

witch cozy authors who kicked my behind regularly, thanks for pushing me to get to The End.

My Southern Charms series is all about family, and my love for my own shows up all throughout the books. Without them, Charli's life might not be that rich.

And finally, to my husband, thanks for being willing to eat cereal for dinner, to let me write while on vacation, and to put up with my obsession in getting the book finished.

About the Author

Bella Falls grew up on the magic of sweet tea, barbecue, and hot and humid Southern days. She met her husband at college over an argument of how to properly pronounce the word *pecan* (for the record, it should be *pea-cawn,* and they taste amazing in a pie). Although she's had the privilege of living all over the States and the world, her heart still beats to the rhythm of the cicadas on a hot summer's evening.

Now, she's taken her love of the South and woven it into a world where magic and mystery aren't the only Charms.

bellafallsbooks.com
contact@bellafallsbooks.com

facebook.com/bellafallsbooks

twitter.com/bellafallsbooks

instagram.com/bellafallsbooks

amazon.com/author/bellafalls

98412469R00162

Made in the USA
Lexington, KY
07 September 2018